Rex's Mate

By
V.S. Morgan

Dedication

To those who asked for more.

Chapter One

Aaron jammed a hand through his hair as agitation mounted. Where the fuck was David? He checked his watch. Midnight. He'd been standing in this parking lot for thirty minutes. The voice mails he'd received sounded urgent, but here he stood in the dark on the ass-end of Hoboken with no brother in sight. The lights and sounds of the nearby traveling carnival did nothing to soothe his nerves.

The messages were the first Aaron had heard from David in nearly a month. Damn, he'd wished he hadn't missed those calls. He had so many questions, like where had his brother been and why he called from an unknown number. They'd always been close, staying in frequent contact even during his brother's tours in Afghanistan. But all that changed when his unit tangled with an IED six months ago, and David returned home with a traumatic brain injury and PTSD. The more Aaron tried to be there for him, the further his brother pushed him away. Aaron had let a few weeks slide, hoping some space would cool the tension between them, but he'd begun to worry. Since he was still listed as his brother's medical guardian, he'd been notified David missed several appointments. In the beginning, Aaron attended all of David's appointments with him, but his uber-independent brother had insisted he could manage them on his own. Damn it, he should have listened to his gut and insisted on going.

"Hey, bro."

He whipped around to see his brother in the shadows about five feet away. Aaron strode toward his twin, taking in his rumpled appearance. David stepped under the street light, illuminating black-and-white hair instead of its normal dark-brown color. His face was waxy, and his features twitched in an agitated tic.

"What happened to you?"

"I'm sorry. They said the treatment would help. Promised it would stop the headaches. The nightmares. The flashbacks." His brother's voice sounded reedy.

"Who said?" Aaron's shock gave way to anger.

"Doctors. They approached me as I was leaving a therapy session. Asked me to be a part of a trial study for a new drug. I was sick for a couple of weeks but began feeling better. Like the old me. They kept giving me meds, and things started to change. My head felt crowded, like someone else was in there trying to communicate with me. I freaked and snuck out. Maybe I'm going crazy."

Aaron's gut twisted at his brother's shattered expression. "Shit. Let's get you to a hospital. No telling what they gave you." He shuddered as the thought of his brother at the mercy of some quacks made his blood run cold.

"No, just let me crash at your place."

A black van pulled up, and four hulking men in ski masks emerged.

"It's them. Run!" David shoved him.

"I'm not leaving you." He yanked his phone from his pocket. He fumbled dialing 911 as they approached. *Shit. Shit. We're screwed.*

One of the men knocked his phone out of his hand and crushed it with the heel of his boot. He frantically scanned the area. No one was around. The urge to run was strong, but there was no way in hell he'd abandon his brother. Aaron swung at him, which the man easily dodged before grabbing him from behind. He squirmed and kicked, but nothing broke the man's iron grip. His chest tightened in fear as he stared at his brother surrounded by the other three, each outweighing him by at least fifty pounds. Even with his Army training, he didn't stand a chance. David kicked the closest one, and the man flew through the air, slamming against the van's side before crumpling to the ground.

Holy shit, what the fuck was that?

"David!" he yelled as another man Tazed his brother.

David fell to the ground, his body jerking from the electrical currents coursing through it.

The man holding Aaron pushed him forward and shoved him into the van. Panic set in when a hood enveloped his head and everything went black.

Chapter Two

Rex loved men. Tall men, short men, little twinks, big hairy bears.... Oh, yeah, he loved a bear every now and then. He'd sampled plenty of what the shifter and human male population had to offer. So, why was he, a self-professed slut, coming home from the club alone despite receiving many offers? *Again.* He hadn't gotten laid in months.

It was all his best friend slash former fuck buddy Hunter's fault. He had to go and find himself a bond mate. Seeing the pair's love made Rex want more. He couldn't settle for meaningless sex. Not after his friend told him about the special connection mates had with the side benefit of out-of-this-world sex.

That sounded pretty damn awesome, but, really, his heart and his wolf wanted someone who'd look at him the way Casey looked at Hunter. A partner to spend the rest of his life with since he'd retired from the gun-for-hire business. But how likely would he find "the one?" Hell, he hadn't even known gay bond mates were possible until Hunter found his little wolf.

He entered the Alpha house. Once he'd joined the Pawlak pack, Casey had insisted he live in the big house with them, but the huge place sometimes felt crowded with the love birds running around.

He passed the kitchen and stopped. Something smelled delicious. Like vanilla ice cream and the cinnamon churros his **mamá** used to make. He strode in and flicked on the lights. Strange, a hint of ocean lingered in the air, despite being over a thousand miles from one. Damn, it reminded him of lazy days on the beach a lifetime ago.

Hearing a rustle, he noticed a tall wire cage without a top. *That's new. Casey must be at it again.* He was always looking after some injured critter or shifter in need. It was funny his kickass friend had mated with such a softie. Rex chuckled. Maybe they should change their pack's name from Pawlak to Marshmallow. He and Hunter better step up their training. Retired or not, they needed to protect the gentle hearts. Technically, that was Casey's dad's job as Alpha, but the dude was old.

The yummy smells came from the cage where something huddled under a blanket. Ah, he must be smelling the fabric softener. Rex crouched down.

"Hey there. Didn't mean to scare you." The blanket rustled and a black-and-white rabbit the size of a small house cat emerged.

"Oh, you're a cute little bunny," he cooed.

His wolf laughed at him.

Yeah, I like fluffy animals, too. Fuck off.

The rabbit stared at him, nose quivering. Poor thing looked banged up. It had fur missing in a few patches and gauze wrapped around one foreleg.

He slowly stuck his finger through the wires of

the cage and rubbed its head between the ears. It nuzzled against him. *So soft.* He chuckled when it licked and gently nibbled his finger.

"Well, I better hit the sack. It's late. Night, bun." He rose, turned off the lights, and strode out of the kitchen.

Off to bed, alone. Damn you, Hunter.

***

Something tickled his ear, and teeth nipped the lobe. Oh, he liked it a bit rough.

"Oh yeah, baby. Bite me again. Harder." Rex opened his eyes, finding himself on his side, face-to-face with the rabbit.

"Fuck." He scrambled back, landing bare-assed on the floor.

Fuck bunny?

His wolf's puzzled response had him crab walking toward the door. How the hell had it gotten in bed with him? *Hunter.* That shithead.

Leaving the rabbit there, Rex shoved onto his feet and stormed upstairs to their room. He opened the door with so much force it slammed against the wall, causing Priss to bark at the end of the bed.

His righteous indignation diminished slightly with Hunter's Glock trained on him. Maybe he needed to rethink how soft the former assassin had gotten. His friend lowered the gun and glared at him.

"What the fuck, Hunter?" He planted his hands on his hips, more confident without a gun pointed at his face.

Casey sat up and rubbed his eyes, his reddish-blond hair standing on end. "What's the naked, crazy man yelling about?"

Hunter covered the little wolf's eyes. Shifters weren't prudes, but he was one possessive fuck now he had a mate. "What's your damage? And go put some clothes on. Casey doesn't need to see your man bits."

"As if you didn't know. I moved here, froze my balls off last winter, and how do you repay that friendship? By putting a rabbit on my bed. That wasn't fucking funny. I could have eaten him." His stomach churned even though his wolf huffed in denial, insulted by the accusation.

No eat. Wolf like bunny.

Yeah, probably too much, you dumb wolf.

"And if it shits on my bed, there will be hell to pay."

Casey shoved Hunter's hand from his eyes. "The rabbit's on your bed?"

"That's what I've been trying to tell you. What a stupid thing to do."

"Fool, I didn't put him there."

"Right, it just Peter Panned out of its cage, hopped all those stairs, and jumped into bed with me." Rex crossed his arms over his chest.

"He," Hunter said.

"Whatever."

"You didn't hurt him, did you?" Casey asked in a panicked voice as he scrambled out of the bed.

Hunter grunted, a scowl on his face, and flung off the blankets to stand. "Stay, Priss," he ordered the dog and led the way out.

"No, I didn't." Rex followed his two equally naked friends to his room.

Casey knelt by the bed. "Hey, Harvey. It's okay.

I'll take you to your cage." He reached for the bunny, but it shied away from him.

"So, where did you find this one, Casey?" Rex smirked while the rabbit continued to ignore the smaller shifter's friendly gestures.

Hunter stood off to the side, his arms crossed. "Harvey's a princess. Garrett and Ryland brought him in. Den Mother requested we care for him until they know more."

Princess was the term their former employer used for targets deemed worthy of rescuing rather than assassinating. Both men and women were called princesses...but bunnies? *Give me a break.*

Rex snorted. "Is the organization so hard up for business they've resorted to rescuing critters?" He shook his head. "Things must have really gone to hell after we retired."

"Let me say this slow so you understand. He. Is. A. Shifter." Hunter glared at him.

"The fuck you say? He can't be a shifter. I asked Den Mother. He said all shifters are predators and the vamp is like 350 years old, so he should know. Besides he doesn't smell like one of us." Rex paused to sniff again. "Smells like rabbit with a bit of human." Along with those other awesome scents, which he was *not* going to mention. Way too much for his brain to handle right now.

"Well, he's special. Den Mother says based on preliminary tests, Harvey is a human-were hybrid," Hunter said.

"No shit. How is that even possible? Humans and shifters can't produce offspring."

"That's the organization's top priority to figure out." Hunter rolled his shoulders.

Yeah, thinking of their old job made him tense, too.

The rabbit evaded Casey's gentle touch by burrowing under the blanket. "Since we don't know his name, we've been calling him Harvey. More personal than 'he,' 'rabbit,' or 'bunny.'"

"Maybe I should tranq him," Hunter said with a frown.

Casey gasped, looking scandalized. "Drugging isn't always the answer."

The big wolf smiled. "Worked with you, baby." He rubbed his mate's shoulder, causing the smaller shifter to moan and lean into his touch.

Unbelievable.

"All right, enough of that shit. I'll get the bunny. Clearly, he likes me or my bed, at least." Rex lifted the blanket off Harvey and held out his hands. The rabbit hopped over, and he scooped him up. Rex tapped down the odd surge of satisfaction the rabbit preferred him.

They trekked downstairs to the kitchen, and he placed Harvey in the cage. The open top made sense now. Didn't want him to be trapped when he shifted.

"Why hasn't he returned to his human form?" Rex said.

"They found him in a lab fire a few days ago. Apparently, he doesn't heal as quickly as we do, and Den Mother thinks he's stuck in his animal state," Hunter said.

"For how long?" Rex asked, dread rising. If a shifter stayed in his animal form too long, he risked losing his humanity forever.

"He doesn't know," Hunter said.

"There are an awful lot of naked butts in my

kitchen. That can't be sanitary." Rex turned to see Hunter's mother standing with her hands on her hips just inside the kitchen. "And is that a rabbit? What have you boys been up to now?"

"Hey, Mom, we're doing a solid for Den Mother."

"Is that man trying to get you back into the business? I'm going to have words with him."

Hunter shook his head. "No, only helping take care of the rabbit."

"Somehow I doubt that's all he wants. Well, go get dressed while I cook breakfast."

"Yes, ma'am. Come on, Casey." Hunter draped a beefy arm around his small mate.

Rex chuckled. "Mr. Big Badass is afraid of his **mamá**." His laugh died in his throat when Mrs. H gave him the skunk eye.

"No sassing in my kitchen, young man, or there won't be any biscuits and gravy for you."

Oh, shit. "Yes, ma'am." He peeked at Harvey one last time before leaving the kitchen.

Chapter Three

That afternoon, Rex hunched under a truck hood, inspecting the carburetor. Scenting Hunter, he glanced sideways as his big friend stopped near the rig.

"Den Mother wants to brief us in twenty."

Rex straightened and wiped his hands on a rag. "What part of being retired does he not understand?"

Hunter frowned, his brows drawn in a grim line. "He needs us. Watch this and decide for yourself. I'm in."

"Casey's okay with that?"

"Yes, he is."

Hunter handed him a thumb drive and a pack of gum. "And have a trash can close by."

Rex straightened to his full height, his wolf bristling. "What, you don't think I can handle it? After all the shit we've seen?"

"I couldn't and had to clean up the floor." His best bud's grin was self-mocking.

Rex relaxed a bit. "Well, then thank you."

"I'll be in the Alpha's den when you're ready." Hunter grasped his shoulder before striding out of the garage.

Rex entered the shop's office and connected the drive to the computer. He grunted but hauled the trash can closer as Ryland's voice and blaring fire alarms came through the speakers.

"Entering the lab now." Ryland's camera feed displayed flashing lights on concrete walls. The ceiling sprinklers doused out flames and shut off when he entered.

Ryland gasped and gagged. "Holy fuck, Ops, are you getting this?"

He'd entered a laboratory full of horrors. Several corpses were laid out on metal tables. Grimaces etched their faces, and their mouths were open in silent screams. *Fuck, they died in agony.* Others were in various stages of dissection. Ryland focused on one cut open from chest to groin. The rib cage appeared cracked open, and intestines hung out from the abdomen. His camera then zoomed in on a corpse with the top of his skull removed. Needles stuck out from the poor bastard's brain. Rex's stomach roiled, and his wolf growled. He heaved into the garbage can. *Jesus.* As soon as he stopped puking, he crossed himself—which he hadn't done since he was a kid. This was truly the worst evil he'd ever seen, and he'd seen plenty.

A loud explosion riveted his attention back to the computer screen.

"I'm okay," Ryland said and continued forward. "Picking up a heartbeat from the next room."

"Abort. Repeat abort now," Ops ordered.

"No, have to find who's alive. May have answers to this freak show."

Ryland progressed into the next room and to a

corner with boxes stacked in front of it. He reached for something behind them.

An unearthly scream sounded, sending a chill down Rex's spine and his wolf whimpered.

"Come on. Let's get you safe." His former teammate's whisper amplified through his mic.

"Ops, I have a rabbit. Extracting now." Ryland cradled a panting Harvey. His fur was singed in spots with an angry burn on his front leg.

Rex shuddered, fighting for control while his wolf howled in savage hatred. *Kill men who hurt bunny.*

He had known this level of rage only once in his life, and an entire Mexican drug cartel had died as a result. After jamming a stick of gum in his mouth, he began to viciously chew.

I'm going to kill these fuckers.

Rex rode his Harley to Alpha house. After giving Casey a curt hello, he joined Hunter in Alek Pawlak's den, claiming the other leather chair facing the large flat screen mounted on the wall. Akio Tamashiro, also known as Den Mother, appeared there.

"Thank you for agreeing to meet. We need all assets on this." Their former leader's normally serene face was pinched, and his eyes were so dark they were black. *Is that pain reflecting from them?* Rex shifted restlessly in his seat, unsettled by their visibly shaken boss. He had been their rock. Now, the time had come to return the favor.

"We'd received intel a group called The Brotherhood was conducting illegal medical experimentation, so I sent a team to investigate. The group fled, setting off explosives to aid their escape. What Ryland found...I've seen before." The vampire grimaced, his usually melodic voice as sharp as glass. "I thought I'd stamped out the evil long ago, but that monster's work lives on."

Rex and Hunter glanced at each other. Who could be responsible for something so horrific?

Den Mother continued but went somewhere Rex hadn't expected. "I was in love once. With a wolf shifter named Erik. We lived in a wooded area, isolated from humans and shifters alike. Our home was small and simple but perfect." He paused, drawing in a deep breath. "One day while I slept, we were attacked. I was left for dead, and Erik was taken."

"Who took him?" Rex asked.

Den Mother's eyes flashed red, and his features hardened. "Nazis. As soon as I recovered, I searched for him, staying in the shadows, as a Japanese man was conspicuous in Europe. Through my connections in the Allied Forces spy network, I learned of experiments being conducted by Josef Mengele."

Mengele, oh fuck.

"We couldn't penetrate the walls of Auschwitz. Once the Soviet Army moved in, we were able to enter. I found Erik...I was too late." Den Mother closed his eyes, and a blood tear streaked down his cheek. "I discovered the research. Not knowing why Erik had supreme strength and healing abilities, Mengele experimented on him. He also poisoned humans with Erik's blood. I destroyed all the data and samples I could find, but Mengele must have taken some when he escaped." He reopened his eyes, glowing red with rage. "I spent many years with Mossad, tracking him in South America. We finally located and killed him in 1979."

So, the story of his accidental drowning off the coast of Brazil had been a cover up.

"You're saying some scientific nut jobs are using Mengele's work to create shifters?" Hunter asked.

"What better way to make super soldiers?"

Fuck.

"What's the plan?" He cracked his knuckles as his wolf paced.

"We're working on the encrypted data now. I have all teams out hunting for The Brotherhood. Once found, they will be destroyed. I want you two involved."

"Sure thing, Den Mother," Hunter said. "What about Harvey?"

"He may hold information key to finding these people if he returns to human form."

"Will it be dangerous to shift?" Rex gulped, thinking of the room full of twisted bodies.

"It's more dangerous for him to remain an animal."

They ended the connection, and Hunter turned to him. "Let's go shoot some shit up."

"Hell, yeah."

They drove out to a remote area of the pack's territory and pulled out their arsenal of weapons. After expending a small fortune of ammo into cans and various targets, Rex's tension eased. Back at the house, he plopped onto the couch and flipped through the TV channels. He stopped on one of the food competition shows he liked.

Harvey jumped onto his lap. His bald spots were gone, and his leg looked nearly healed. Rex stroked his fur and commented on the show as he watched. Sensing the rabbit's contentment, his wolf calmed.

He heard a click and turned to see Casey with his phone. "Too cute. I couldn't resist taking a picture."

Rex shrugged in indifference, but smiled when his own phone pinged signaling Casey had sent it to him, as well.

Chapter Four

Rex woke to a furry body sitting on him, little nails digging into his skin. He opened his eyes. Yep, Harvey perched on his bare chest even though he'd been placed in the kitchen for the night.

"I like you, bud, but this is too kinky, even for me. You want to share my bed, you need to be a man." He stroked the long, velvet-soft ears. "Can you understand me? I want to meet you. Maybe you just don't know how." Rex placed the rabbit on the mattress and stood. "Do you see me? A man, right? Well, I'm going to think about my wolf. Watch closely."

Rex concentrated, and, within seconds, he shifted to his wolf form.

Harvey went as rigid as a statue.

His wolf chuckled when a pungent smell emitted. *Bunny pooed on bed.*

Yeah, that's your bed too, dummy.

Wolf stopped laughing. *Bunny scared?* He whined, lowered himself onto the floor, and belly crawled a few feet. Rising to place his muzzle on the edge of the bed, he whined again and swished his tail.

Harvey wiggled his nose, and his ears perked up. He hopped over, and Rex's wolf nuzzled against his fur. The rabbit rubbed his chin along Rex's head, marking him with his delicious cinnamon-and-vanilla scent. Fierce possession rolled through him, and his wolf growled. *Mate. Bunny mine.*

Fuck. No denying it now. He shifted and petted Harvey's back. "So that's how it works. Think about being a man again, and I'll be here waiting for you."

The rabbit scratched an ear with a big hind foot. Rex sighed and picked him up. "Well, you think about it while I change these sheets."

Setting the rabbit on the floor, he stripped off the linens and replaced them with fresh ones.

"Much better, huh, li'l bun?" He glanced down.

No Harvey. Rex hung his head out his doorway, wondering where the little guy had gotten off to just in time to see Harvey shoot past with Priss on his heels.

"Priss, no!" He dove and snatched the Pomeranian to his chest.

"They're only playing. He wouldn't hurt Harvey," Casey said, coming down the hall.

The dog twisted free and gave Rex the "bitch, please" look.

The bunny raced by and jumped, twisting and kicking his back feet out with so much air time Michael Jordan would have been proud.

"Whoa."

Casey laughed. "That means he's happy."

"Oh, cool," Rex said, but sadness welled. If Harvey was happy as a rabbit, would he ever become a man again?

He spent the day trying to shake the unease threatening to overwhelm him. What if his mate remained an animal? Rex would care for him, providing the best life possible, of course, but he ached to know the man hidden within. He hit the gym, taped up, and went to it on the heavy bag. He quit after an hour, his punches becoming sloppy when his thoughts returned to his mate.

Striping out of his clothes, he shifted. After running his wolf to the point of exhaustion, Rex went home. Returning to human form, he stumbled to his room, flopped into bed, and conked out.

Rex was having the best dream ever. Cinnamon, vanilla, and the sea surrounded him. He licked a smooth shoulder, enjoying the salty taste of man as his dick edged along the crease of the pert ass pressed against him.

"What the fuck." A strong New York accent broke through his sleepy haze, and the warm body jerked away. A foot rudely caught him in the balls.

"Ow!" he howled. This was no dream. He squinted, holding his nuts, trying not to barf. Shit, the dude was strong. Rex had taken a hit or two to the boys before, but it'd never hurt this bad.

The naked guy scrambled toward the closet. Rex had never seen anything like him. His hair stood out in a wild black-and-white combo, and his body was long and lean. He had large eyes, a long slim nose, and full lips drawn back from perfect teeth in a menacing snarl. Rex rubbed his two working brain cells together and came up with *Harvey*.

He raised a hand and grunted in pain. "It's okay. Just a misunderstanding."

"Who are you? What are you doing in my bed?"

Harvey's eyes flashed.

"Actually, this is my room."

"How did I get here? Where's David?" Harvey grabbed the camo jacket off the closet door knob and shrugged into it.

"Hold on." Rex leaned over to snag his phone, barely suppressing an unmanly whimper. Thumbing the number, he waited for his friend to answer.

"Hunter, princess is awake. Need back up." He ended the call and tossed the phone onto the bed without waiting for a response. Easing into an upright position, he climbed off the mattress and hobbled over to turn on the light.

Harvey blinked before grabbing the baseball bat leaning against the wall. "Stay away from me, meathead."

So fierce and beautiful.

Rex's wolf rumbled with pride. *Mate.*

Aaron clutched the bat tight, ready to knock the shit out of the buff, naked dude if he took one step closer with that freaking salami of his.

He searched for exits. The brick shithouse blocked the door. The window would take too long to open, leaving him vulnerable to attack from behind. He maneuvered his back to a wall and waited. He'd get around this dickhead and out the door.

His legs trembled, and fatigue swept through him. Fuck, his head hurt. What had happened? He'd been talking to his brother in that Jersey parking lot.... "Where the fuck is David?"

"I don't know anyone named David. I'm not going to hurt you. Just put the bat down," the large man said, pointing to the floor.

"Like I'm going to trust you. Do I look stupid?" Aaron glared at him.

The big guy shook his head. "No, of course not. I want to help you."

"Start by telling me what's going on," he demanded.

"You were in an accident. A fire. You're recovering here."

He frowned in confusion. "In a house and not the hospital?"

Dude nodded. "It's safer here."

"Yeah, so much safer with your dick almost up my ass." Aaron snorted.

The big man blushed. "Like I said, a misunderstanding. My name's Rex. What's yours?"

"Wouldn't you like to know," he sneered. Yet, this guy seemed familiar. His voice maybe. Something inside told him he wasn't in danger, that this man wouldn't harm him.

A huge black guy stormed in. Even bigger than Rex, he looked like one mean fucker. Aaron tightened his grip on the bat.

"Okay, you two, out. You're scaring him," said the latest arrival, a short, reddish-blond haired man.

The black dude grunted in response.

The smaller guy frowned. "Hunter, ask your mom to bring some food and water. He's probably starving after shifting."

Shifting?

"But this is my room," Rex whined as he grabbed the phone off the king-sized bed.

The little guy merely pointed toward the door, and the two left with a huff. It was almost comical watching the two goons taking orders from a dude with floppy ginger hair and a baby face.

"No one's going to hurt you. How about you put the bat down and we talk," the other man said in a soothing voice.

"Talk first." Aaron was no dummy, although he could probably take this guy out easy.

"I'm Casey. You were rescued from a fire. We don't know anything else about you." Casey opened a dresser drawer, rummaged around, and pulled out a pair of shorts. He held them out, but Aaron ignored them.

"Did you find my brother?"

Casey shook his head. "Sorry, you were the only person there. If you tell us what your name is, we can help you find him."

Aaron doubted that. Snatches of memory filtered through his mind. The abduction near the carnival. Then being so sick he'd thought he would die. He needed to get out of here.

"I need to leave right now." He gripped the bat, ready to do battle if need be.

"Honey, there will be time for that later. Right now, you need to get back in bed and eat," a middle-aged black woman said from the doorway. She had a tray with something that smelled really good. His stomach cramped with sharp hunger pains. His knees wobbled, threatening to give out. Damn it, he couldn't stand much longer.

Staring into the woman's eyes, he only saw kindness there. He dropped the bat and inched closer. Casey placed the shorts he'd been holding onto the bed and moved toward the door. The woman nodded to the redhead, and he left.

Aaron shuffled forward and yanked on the shorts, his need to remain vigilant overriding the urge to modestly turn as he did so. He tightened the drawstring so they wouldn't fall off his narrow hips.

"That's right. Climb on in. I've got a nice broth for you."

He had no reason to trust her, yet he obeyed her request. Like the others, she seemed oddly familiar. Beautiful with espresso skin and high cheekbones, the woman had a dancer's body. Her posture was regal despite her casual clothes.

She set the tray on the nightstand and adjusted the blankets around him, just like his *nonna* did when he was a child. She handed him the tray before settling in the wooden chair next to the bed.

"My name is Delonda, but most folks call me Del or Mrs. H."

"I'm Aaron." He stared longingly at the bowl. What if it was drugged? He glanced into her knowing eyes.

"I can taste it first, if you'd like," she said, her voice gentle.

Unease warred with something deep telling him it was okay. He took a sip and closed his eyes. *Amazing.* It seemed like years since he'd last eaten. He slurped the broth until his spoon scraped the bottom of the bowl. Then he drank the water provided.

He tensed at a throat clearing. A girl who appeared to be around his age stood in the doorway. She held another glass of water. "Thought he'd need another."

"Thank you, honey. Aaron, this is my daughter Mikaela."

A mini version of her mother, yet her eyes were even softer, kinder somehow. Mikaela entered carefully like she didn't want to spook him.

After he finished the second glass, he settled back against the headboard, suddenly drained.

"Try to get some rest," Mrs. H said as she ushered her daughter out and turned off the light.

He burrowed into the pillow and smiled. It smelled of peppermint, his *bubbe's* latkes, and pine. Memories of long ago holidays swirled around him as he drifted off to sleep.

Chapter Five

"So, this is where you've been hiding." Hunter leaned against the Mustang Rex had been tinkering with the last few hours.

"He hates me. Called me a meathead." Rex sighed and threw the wrench he'd been using into the toolbox. His wolf whimpered in misery.

"You can have any man you want, yet you're moping around because of a skinny, mouthy guy. What gives?"

"He's my mate."

"Shut the fuck up."

"I'm not shitting you. He smells amazing to me, and my wolf insists he's our mate. What if it isn't mutual? He's a hybrid after all." His stomach plummeted.

"Well, he's been through a lot. What would you have done if you'd woken up in a strange place with some random dude all over you?" Hunter raised a hand. "Never mind answering that, I'm sure you would have loved it."

Maybe in the past.

"He can't hate you too much. I hear he's still wearing your jacket like a security blanket."

Rex cocked his head and glanced at his friend. "Yeah? How's he doing?"

"Resting after he calmed down and ate. I'd swear he's a wolverine shifter. They're real assholes. You'd think a cute bunny would be nicer."

"Wolverines are crazy in bed."

Hunter rolled his eyes.

"What should I do?"

"Well, you need to stop hiding in the shop first of all. Show him you're not a complete dickhead."

"Thanks for the awesome pep talk, Dr. Phil."

"You're welcome. Oh, and his name is Aaron, but he didn't give up any other info. Den Mother's got people on it."

***

Aaron peered through his lashes as the large man slid into the room. Rex was stealthy, but his rich scent permeated the air, and Aaron's dick twitched in interest. He wrinkled his brow. *Really?* Now, he was turned on by this lunkhead?

The big dude carried a few shopping bags with high-end store names printed on them. He placed them on the dresser by the foot of the bed. A small, white dog ran in and jumped onto the bed. It pawed at Aaron and whined.

"Priss," Rex hissed and grabbed for the Pomeranian. He paused when their gazes locked.

Busted.

Picking up the dog, Rex stepped back. "Sorry he woke you. Just leaving you some clothes and stuff."

The big guy shifted Priss to one arm and hooked a thumb over his shoulder toward the dresser.

Aaron sat up and continued to eye him. He kept his face stony while his insides were in turmoil. On one hand, he didn't trust this stranger, and, on the other, he couldn't shake knowing him on some level. Heat flamed at the large man's proximity, his enticing scent a potent tug to Aaron's libido. The fact he was damn attractive wasn't helping matters either. He took in the thick dark hair, soulful chocolate-brown eyes, and chiseled features. Rex had a powerful body like those MMA fighters David admired. Aaron hadn't understood the appeal until now.

"I'm sorry about last night." Rex rubbed the back of his neck in a gesture Aaron found oddly endearing. The large man wasn't so sure of himself.

"This is your room." The numbness in his heart overpowered any guilt he might have felt.

"Yeah, but stay as long as you like. No sweat." The big guy gestured nonchalantly with his free hand.

Aaron scratched his ear. "How did I end up here?"

"Don't know. You were in the kitch— Downstairs. Maybe got turned around. It's a big house, and you're still recovering."

Rex was hiding something, and it put Aaron on edge. His head felt crowded like someone else tried to chime in, too. Hadn't David said he'd experienced the same thing? Aaron's chest constricted. Had those doctors given him the same drugs? He couldn't remember.

"How are you feeling?" Rex's concern surprised him, but he refused to show weakness.

"Much better thanks," he said in a curt tone.

Rex nodded. "I'll let Casey know you're awake. He'll bring you some food. The bathroom's across the hall."

"Close the door when you leave, please."

"Sure thing," Rex said and left.

Aaron jumped out of bed and dug through the bags. Should he be worried that everything was in his size? Had Rex measured him while he slept? After removing the jacket, he pulled on a fitted T-shirt over the borrowed shorts from the night before. He padded to the bathroom. After he relieved himself, Aaron glanced at his reflection in the mirror. *Fuck.* He touched his hair—black and white just like David's.

A memory exploded in his head. His brother hovering over him. "They're leaving. Now's your chance to get away. I'll distract them."

David picked him up in his arms, seeming enormous to Aaron's fevered brain. His brother must have put him down at some point because his next clear memory was of him running.

Fire. Scared. Can't breathe. Pain.

Aaron dry heaved into the toilet. He waited until the shuddering stopped before turning on the sink faucet and splashing water on his face.

Need to get out of here. Have to find David. Danger.

Returning to the bedroom, he pushed off the shorts and quickly slid on briefs, jeans, and socks. After putting on tennis shoes, he shrugged into the oversized camouflaged coat. His mind warred with the need to flee and the whispered reassurance he was safe here.

"Oh, good. You're up and looking much better."

Casey stood in the doorway with a tray. Priss sat at his feet.

Aaron shoved the smaller man against the wall, causing the tray and everything on it to crash onto the hardwood floor, food splattering.

"What have you done to me?" Aaron spat out.

"We wouldn't hurt you. We're protecting you," Casey said.

"What day is this?"

"October fifth."

Shit, he'd been gone over a month. *School.* Would he lose his scholarship? *Fuck.* "Where am I?

"Minnesota."

How the hell had he gotten here? "Give me your phone." He patted the other man down searching for it.

"Don't have it on me. You need to let me go. I want to help, but he will kill you if you hurt me."

"Who? The dog?" Aaron glanced at Priss in disbelief.

"Hunter."

The fierce black dude. Yeah, that he could believe.

Fisting Casey's T-shirt, he hauled him to the closet and thrust him inside. Needle-like teeth sank into his ankle. *Fuck.*

"Make him stop. I don't want to hurt him," Aaron bit out, resisting the urge to shake the pooch off.

"Priss, release." The dog obeyed the command as well as the one to come to his owner.

Aaron shut the closet doors and tied them closed with a thin towel. His eyes met the other man's through the narrow slats.

"I'm sorry." True regret tinged his words. He turned and heaved the window open.

"No, it's not safe out there. You smell like prey." Casey called and pounded on the closet doors.

What the hell does that mean?

Second floor, no problem. He'd gotten plenty of practice running away from foster care. After climbing down the drain pipe most of the way, he jumped. He briefly surveyed the rural surroundings. Nothing but woods on this side of the house. *Where the hell am I?* He trembled with fear and anger. Why did he have to be so impulsive? He had no money, no phone, and no plan.

Sounds came from behind him, and he sprinted into the woods, **adrenaline** coursing through his body. Driven by a weird euphoria, he ran harder, his stride lengthening, his breath visible in the cold air. He'd done track in school and still jogged for exercise, but now he was stronger and faster than ever before. *Amazing!*

Suddenly, a voice inside his head yelled "freeze." He came to a jarring stop and listened. Every noise was amplified loud and clear, even over the sound of his racing heart. Fuck, were those wolves howling? Wolves had a bad rep, but he knew they didn't attack humans. *You smell like prey.* Casey's words echoed through his head.

A pack of wolves crested the rise. Five of them. One sniffed the air and growled. They loped down the hill toward him.

Run!

Listening to the inner command, he darted off. Without looking, he knew they'd picked up speed. Aaron tripped and fell, sprawling on the moist ground. *Shit.* He scrambled to his feet. His energy was fading fast. Glancing around, he surveyed his options. The wolves would reach him before he got to the nearest climbable tree. He spotted a patch of sticker bushes, but he'd never fit there.

Think small. Think rabbit, a voice in his head thundered.

He did as it said. His body tingled with a weird energy, like static shock only stronger. Everything got huge, and he found himself buried in clothing. Struggling, he kicked loose and dashed to the bushes, squeezing into a hole that seemed ridiculously tiny. He moved farther into the spikey vines when the wolves pawed and dug at them.

A huge, brown wolf appeared, snarling at the others. They flipped onto their backs, exposing their bellies. The larger animal huffed at them, and they yipped and slunk off. Standing a few feet from Aaron's shelter, the big wolf watched them go before swinging his head toward the bushes. The wolf sniffed and made a grunting sound.

Aaron quivered. Part of him feared the huge predator; the other was relieved. Again the sense of familiarity washed over him. He smelled like.... No. How was that possible?

The wolf's body shimmered, and in its place stood a very naked Rex. *Holy shit!*

"It's okay. I'll take you home," the large man said as he hunkered down. Smiling gently, he made a coaxing gesture with his hand.

Knowing he couldn't stay there forever, he hesitantly emerged, and Rex's smile broadened, dimples on full display. The man was positively enormous as he bundled Aaron in his camo jacket and picked him up. Exhausted, Aaron decided he'd rest in his arms for just a little while.

The large man carried him through the woods and out to a gravel road. Hunter and Casey were waiting in an SUV. He trembled as Rex climbed in the back. As Hunter drove, Rex talked to Aaron in a soothing tone. He felt calm flow through him, inhaling the big guy's wonderful scent. Seeking the strongest concentration of it, he burrowed into Rex's armpit, and the other man laughed.

"What the fuck do you find funny about this situation?" Hunter growled.

"He tickled me." Rex caressed Aaron's back. "It's okay. You can change any time. I'm here for you," the large man murmured. "Just remember to think about being in your human form."

Human form?

Yes, think man, not bunny, the voice in his head said. *Focus.*

He experienced the odd prickling sensation again. Suddenly, Rex was smaller, or he was bigger.

Absolutely drained, he struggled to climb off the other man's naked lap.

"Shh. I've got you," Rex said, adjusting the jacket to better cover Aaron's bare body before cradling him to his chest.

His foggy brain replayed what had happened. Rex had been a wolf. And he'd changed to-to...what? His mind rebelled against the absurd possibility he'd changed into a rabbit.

The SUV came to a stop in front of the house. He tried to get out on his own power but stumbled as soon as his feet touched the ground.

Rex grabbed his arm, steadying him. "Let me

carry you."

"I won't be packed around like some stupid bride," he sniped, furious at his weakness.

"Of course not. For you, I'll do a manly carry," Rex said and hoisted him up and over his shoulder, placing a large, warm hand firmly on Aaron's bare butt, stopping his squirming.

The big guy chuckled at his indignant hiss. He pinched Rex's equally bare ass, which earned him another chuckle.

"You can't hold me prisoner. I'm going to have all of you arrested!" he yelled when they reentered the house.

Rex carried him into the living room and deposited him on a sofa before sitting next to him. Hunter stood with his arms crossed, glaring down at Aaron from his impressive height.

"Princess or no, you lay a hand on Casey again, I'll drop kick you through the wall."

Aaron gulped and shuddered, no doubt in his mind the man would do it.

Rex growled low and drew him close to his side, the scents of peppermint and evergreen saturating in the air. The savory aroma of potato and onion latke soothed Aaron as he hid his face against the other man's neck.

"Hunter, he's scared, and threatening him isn't going to help matters. Besides, if he'd wanted to hurt me, he would have," Casey said, draping a blanket on Aaron and Rex.

"Thank you," he mumbled, and the redhead smiled reassuringly.

A man with silvery-blond hair and hard blue eyes entered. He looked like an older, badass version of

Casey. Aaron straightened.

The man flicked Hunter a quelling look. "Aaron is our guest. He deserves to know why we're keeping him here."

The cold, blue gaze locked on him. "My name is Aleksander Pawlak, Alpha of this pack. We were asked to care for you after you were found in a laboratory in a remote area outside of Buffalo." The man's expression softened. "Whatever was done to you allows you to change into an animal."

"Is that how he changed into a wolf?" His voice sounded like gravel.

Aleksander shook his head. "We were born this way. We're wolf shifters."

"I'm a shifter, too?" *Shit, it was real.*

"Yes, a rabbit." The older man's features were pinched.

"Out of all the animals in the world, why did it have to be a rabbit?" Aaron tugged at his crazy hair.

"I don't know. Natural shifters are all predators."

"This is so fucked up. My brother David is out there somewhere. I have to find him."

Sympathy shone in Aleksander's eyes. "I'm sorry, son. It's not safe for you to leave. Humans can't know you exist. It's best you stay here."

"What about the wolves that chased me?"

"An unfortunate incident, I'm afraid. The teens were confused by your scent. The pack has been told you're under my protection. You have my word no harm will come to you."

Those were only teenagers? "But my brother...."

"My old boss will help us find him. Can you remember anything about the lab? Did anyone mention names or another location?" Rex asked.

He shook his head. "I don't remember much. It's all so blurry. I'm sorry." He slumped against the other man in exhaustion.

Aleksander turned to Rex. "Take him upstairs to rest. We'll talk later."

Aaron numbly allowed the large man to carry him upstairs. He barely noticed being placed on the bed before fatigue overtook him.

**

He stared at Rex. The big guy was stretched out on the uncomfortable-looking wooden chair, one arm tucked behind his head like a pillow, his face relaxed in sleep, and his lips forming a sexy pout. Aaron's gaze trailed over the large body in repose, taking in all those muscles. He knew plenty of macho Italian men, and he loathed testosterone-laden dumbshits. But this Latin stud really cranked him up. Rex's shirt was bunched, exposing washboard abs. He gaped, mesmerized by the considerable bulge showcased by the track pants drawn tight. *Fuck, he's hot.* His eyes shifted to another, significantly smaller bulge in Rex's pants. A set of keys in his pocket.

Did he dare? He stared at the other man for a few indecisive minutes before approaching. He dropped to his knees, barely breathing.

Rex's package was even more impressive close up. The scents of pine, peppermint, and potato latkes he'd come to associate with the wolf shifter were stronger, as well. He licked his lips, fighting the urge to rub his face in the large man's crotch. Steadying his breath, he slowly reached for the pocket. His fingers skimmed the fabric....

"See something you want?"

Aaron jerked back, his gaze snapping to Rex's face. The shifter's eyes burned molten gold under half-mast lids. So different from their normal chocolate-brown color. *Wolf eyes.*

"Yeah, your keys," he sputtered.

Rex smirked, his eyes calling him a liar. "Oh, *guapo*, you don't want those keys."

He called me handsome. Focus, damn it. "I do. I need to find David."

"Where would you start?" Rex straightened, his movements graceful for a large man.

"I'd go to New York." Aaron scooted toward the bed, desperate for distance from this potent man.

Rex shook his head. "They're long gone. Stay here. I have what you need."

Aaron stared at him in disbelief. Could this guy's ego be any bigger?

"I meant I'm assisting in the search. Some shifters have special talents. Mine is tracking."

"Tracking. Not a master in the sack?" Damn, his mouth could be his worst enemy.

Rex chuckled. "Oh, I've got amazing skills there, too. Just let me know and I'll be happy to demonstrate."

"Not in this lifetime, wolfman."

The other man responded with a cocky smirk, complete with one of those freaking dimples.

Fucker. He pressed his lips together, resisting the urge to smile. Aaron stood and caught his jarring reflection in the dresser mirror. The momentary lightness Rex evoked was snuffed out like a candle.

I'm a freak.

Chapter Six

Rex passed Mrs. H in the hallway. She shook her head. Aaron had stopped eating and barely acknowledged his existence. He'd hoped she would have better luck.

This needed to stop. He couldn't lose his mate. He called Den Mother. Without a hello, Akio said, "I heard your princess made a run for it. Spirit is good. Means he's strong."

"I'm worried about him. He's not eating."

"Aaron's grieving. He was forcefully taken from everything he knows. Even his own body is alien to him. There's so much to process and accept."

"What can I do? Akio, he's my mate."

"Be there for him as he works through this. We've completed our report. His name is Aaron Giovanni Fischer, age twenty-three, from Brooklyn, New York. Only living family member is David Angelo Fischer, his identical twin brother. Both were reported missing a month ago."

Rex thought about the room full of corpses. "Have the police connected all the missing people?"

"No, The Brotherhood deviated from their MO

with the Fischers. The others were homeless or prostitutes from multiple states. While David was vulnerable as an unemployed disabled vet, Aaron was well-established at his school and in the music community. He would be missed. I'm sending you his file now."

"I'll review it. Any information on The Brotherhood's new location?"

"No. I'm hoping Aaron can help. Ryland and I will be there in two hours."

"Good. See you soon."

Rex ended the call and accessed the file. He paused on the cover page. It was one thing to read a target's report, but this was an invasion of his mate's privacy. But if he knew more about Aaron, maybe he'd find a way to earn his trust. After debating for a second or two, he skimmed the contents.

Aaron's heritage was Italian and Jewish Hungarian. Rex grinned. The holidays must have been interesting at his house. His smile disappeared as he continued to read. Aaron's parents had died in a car accident. They'd been broadsided by a drunk driver and died on impact. The eight-year-old twins had been badly injured. Aaron remained in the hospital for five months and endured strenuous rehab to walk again. Rex winced, realizing how close he'd come to never meeting his mate.

The twins lived with their Italian grandparents until they were fourteen. The Mancinis had passed within a short time of each other, the grandmother from cancer and the grandfather from heart failure. With no other family living, the brothers were placed in the system and bounced around a number of group and foster homes.

Aaron had been a good student despite moving from school to school and serving time in a juvenile detention facility. Before his abduction, he'd been a grad student at Juilliard. There were several notations of guest solo performances and other musical accomplishments, all indicating he was a brilliant violinist.

His mate had already overcome so much in his young life. He was a survivor. Rex prayed his strength would serve him now.

***

Aaron rolled over at the double tap on the door. Rex poked his head in.

"There are a few people here to meet you."

He sat up as Rex entered followed by two men. One was tall, with all-American good looks, the other shorter, with jet-black hair and Asian features. Both were attractive, yet neither sparked his interest like Rex.

"This is my former boss, Akio. We call him Den Mother. His group is looking for David."

That had his full attention.

"And this is Ryland. He's the one who found you."

"Thank you." Aaron touched his now healed arm. "I probably would have died there if it hadn't been for you."

Ryland's smile gleamed with a large display of teeth. "My pleasure," he said, his tone deep and suggestive.

Is he flirting with me? He shivered, sensing the predatory vibes rolling off the man.

Rex grunted and positioned himself between Aaron and Ryland.

"Why don't the two of you wait outside," Akio instructed the men eying each other. Once they'd cleared out, he sat on the chair next to the bed.

"Why do they call you Den Mother?"

"Because I always look after my boys." Akio frowned. "I'm very sorry for all you've gone through, Aaron. We're still decrypting the files, but a group known as The Brotherhood is responsible."

"What did they do to us?"

"They injected you with a super virus, which drastically altered your DNA."

"So, it's permanent."

"Yes."

"Why would they do this?"

Akio met his gaze. "I know about your family history. About your grandfather. This will be difficult to hear, but The Brotherhood developed this virus based on Josef Mengele's work. He attempted to make super soldiers from shifter DNA. The Brotherhood created the virus with the remaining sample."

Fuck. Nausea swept through him.

"Super soldier bunnies?" Aaron snarked, struggling for control.

"The original sample had degraded, requiring animal DNA. Rabbits are easy to study and control in a laboratory environment. Once their experimentation was successful, they planned to adapt the virus to include predator DNA."

"How can anyone be so evil?"

"My organization will not stop until they've been destroyed."

"I want to help, but I don't really remember anything except being taken."

Akio nodded. "They gave you powerful drugs, so it's not surprising your memory was affected." He paused. "I have a special talent, which allows me to see another's memories. If I viewed yours, it could provide clues as to where they've taken David."

"Are you a shifter, too?"

"No, I'm a vampire."

Aaron covered his neck with his hands. His body quivered as the rabbit banged around inside him in a panic.

Akio laughed softly. "You're quite safe, my young friend. Rex wouldn't have left you alone with me otherwise." The vampire waited patiently, his face serene. "Or I could have him come back if you'd feel more comfortable."

Aaron didn't want the big shifter babying him. He took a deep breath and released his neck. "Will you see all my memories?"

"I can control my abilities and will only look for memories related to The Brotherhood."

"Are you going to do the Vulcan mind meld thing with me?"

The vampire chuckled. "No, but I get the best results through touch. May I have your hand?"

Akio gently cradled his outstretched hand between both of his own. His hands were warmer than he expected. Weren't vamps supposed to be cold?

"Think about when you were abducted."

He did as instructed, his chest tight. Akio closed his eyes and remained silent for several minutes. Aaron's foot thumped on the bed as his thoughts raced. How long would this take? Would Akio see his past? Regardless, it was the best chance of finding David.

At last, the vampire reopened his eyes and released Aaron's hand.

"Did you see anything?"

"Yes, a name and images of some of the men. Thank you. We'll find your brother."

He gulped. "Do you really think he's still alive?"

"Yes, I don't believe they will harm him. Only the two of you survived the virus, and without you in their possession, David is even more valuable." Akio stood. "I know he's rough around the edges, but Rex is a good man. You can trust him. He's fiercely loyal, and he would kill for you."

He said this as if it were the greatest honor. *What kind of world had Rex lived in?*

***

Ryland leaned against a hallway wall while Rex paced, agitated to leave his mate's side even if Aaron made it clear he wasn't wanted there. That hurt more than Rex wanted to admit. He glanced at the other man.

"I saw the video. Thanks for getting him out of there."

"Just doing my thing, but damn, if I'd known he'd turn out to be such a cutie, I'd have kept him for myself," Ryland said in his deep Southern drawl.

Possessive instincts on overload, Rex got up in his face. "Keep your filthy paws off, Ry, or I will end you."

The other shifter retreated a step and raised his

hands in surrender. "Whoa, easy there. I didn't know you'd staked a claim. Not your style."

"He's my mate."

"Wow. Congrats," Ryland said with a wistful expression. "So...is his brother gay?"

"Hell if I know." Because he had a mate who hadn't shared shit with him. And fuck it, that stung like a bitch. Rex's attention moved to Den Mother approaching.

"His memories provided some valuable details. I'll know more when we return to base. Once we process the information, I'll update you. I want you on rotation."

"Yes, sir."

"Aaron is a well-suited mate for you. Remember to be patient." With that comment, Den Mother strode down the hall. Rex sighed in relief when Ryland followed.

Hearing a crash, he rushed into the bedroom. Aaron slumped against the dresser, his hands bleeding from smashing the mirror. Rex's heart lurched at the anger and pain reflected in his mate's eyes. He reached out, wanting to comfort. His mate flinched.

"They took everything from me. My life, my brother, my music." Aaron's face crumpled. "No!" His body shimmered as he shifted. Trapped by clothing, the rabbit screamed, more in rage than fear. The hairs on the back of Rex's neck stood up at the eerie sound. With gentle hands, he helped Aaron get free. His mate darted frantically around the room, careening into the furniture.

"Aaron, stop." Rex's words were ignored, and the rabbit bounced off the trash can and slid across the smooth hardwood floor leaving a bloody streak.

"*Basta!*"

The rabbit shifter froze, panting.

"Enough. You're going to hurt yourself more than you already have."

He squatted and slowly reached out a hand. Aaron's rabbit jerked back and bared his teeth. Rex waited, knowing any sudden moves would set the bunny scurrying again. After a while his mate hopped over. *Thank fuck.* Rex scooped the rabbit up and carried him to the bed. After placing the bunny on the mattress, Rex settled on his side next to him and stroked his fur.

He tsked softly at the bloody paw prints on the sheets. "Now I have to change the sheets again. Mrs. H will be shocked I'm doing laundry twice in one week."

The rabbit burrowed against his side.

"Shh. It's going to be okay. I know about your life. What you've been through. You're so strong. You can do this." He murmured nonsense in Spanish as he continued to pet the trembling body. Gradually, the rabbit shifter calmed.

When Aaron returned to human form, Rex expected him to move away, but Aaron huddled against his chest. He wrapped his arms around his mate's slender frame.

"How could they do this to us? My grandfather almost died in Auschwitz. David's a soldier. It must be killing him." Aaron broke down with a sob.

Rex held him tightly through the mother of ugly cries. He crooned crap in Spanish while his shirt absorbed the flood of angry tears. A part of him acknowledged how wonderful it felt to hold his mate, his scent surrounding him.

Eventually, the sobs turned to sniffles as he stroked Aaron's super soft hair. He paused when his mate stiffened. "What did you mean when you said you knew about my life?"

"I read your background file."

"It's not enough I'm a prisoner here, but you invaded my privacy. What about my sealed juvie record. Did you see that, too?"

Rex couldn't lie. Not to his mate. "Yes."

"Fucker." Aaron shoved his chest and rolled over, turning his back to him.

Rex sighed and covered the rabbit shifter's naked body with a blanket. Having a mate was damn hard. Casey hadn't given Hunter this much trouble. He pushed the thoughts aside, knowing it wasn't fair to compare the two. Their upbringing and personalities couldn't have been more different. He'd just have to be patient like Den Mother said. Unfortunately, patience wasn't a quality he was known for.

He called Mikaela and asked her to bring some food. His mate ignored him when he carried the tray over.

"You need to eat."

Aaron didn't respond, and Rex suppressed a frustrated growl.

"Look, I know you're awake. Your breathing gives you away." He paused and still no response. "I get this is tough to handle, but if you don't eat, you'll die."

Aaron flopped over with a huff. "Drama queen much?"

Well, at least he'd gotten a response. He understood anger and would take it over silence any day.

"Your body isn't used to shifting. It takes a toll. Your metabolism is working overtime compared to a human. So yes, you'll grow weak and die if you don't eat on a regular basis."

"Would that be so horrible? I'm a freaking rabbit," Aaron retorted.

"Hey, so shit happened. You need to be strong for David. Would he be wallowing around like a little baby? I highly doubt it."

Aaron glared, but he sat up. "Fine. I'll eat if it gets you off my case."

Rex inwardly cheered but snarked back. "Yes, Your Highness." He handed Aaron the tray.

His wolf was marginally satisfied Aaron ate. A deep, possessive urge to hand feed his mate, ensuring he was properly nourished, swept through Rex, but he doubted Aaron would be thrilled with that level of attention. Probably get bit if he tried. He stifled a grin. Might be worth it.

"Is there a way to control changing?"

"It gets easier with time and practice." Rex sat on the chair by the bed.

"Is it possible to never shift again?"

"When an animal gets trapped, it becomes difficult to manage. May pop out when you least want it to. Ask Casey, he repressed his wolf for years."

"Really? Why?"

"He was raised around humans. Had to protect his identity or he would have been exploited for his abilities."

"What kind of abilities?"

"Besides shifting, we have enhanced senses, speed, strength, and we don't get typical human illnesses or diseases, so we have a much longer life span."

"I have all that."

Rex nodded. "I bet you run faster than we do in human form."

"How is it possible for a person to get so small?"

"Den Mother could describe it better, but what allows us to transform into our animals—the bone and muscle structure, hair and teeth—also contracts and expands our mass. Can you imagine a male grizzly bear shifter wandering around in human form over seven feet tall and weighing more than five hundred pounds? Not good for the human body and would make us dangerously conspicuous in the human world."

"Crazy." Aaron scratched his ear and yawned wide as Rex took the tray and set it on the dresser. He started shucking off his clothes.

"What are you doing?" Aaron stared at him with wide eyes.

"I'm not looking forward to another crick in my neck from sleeping in the chair again. I'll be more comfortable in wolf form on the floor."

"I'm sorry I took your room...your bed. I can stay somewhere else. I promise I won't try to run again." Aaron's features bunched, and his eyes darkened.

"I'm going to keep you safe. Even from yourself."

Aaron glanced at his hands and gasped. "I'm almost completely healed."

"Yes, but I strongly recommend you don't go around punching any more mirrors. 'Sides, it's bad luck."

His mate rolled his eyes. "Like my luck is so great to begin with."

Rex shifted. Elated to see their mate, his wolf ignored Aaron's prickliness.

Mate. Mine.

"May I touch you?" Aaron's voice held a note of awe, which did wonders for his deflated ego.

His wolf all but tripped over himself, coming closer. His mate reached out a trembling hand and ran it along the side of his head before scratching the underside of his jaw and behind his ears.

Rex's wolf woofed his pleasure and licked Aaron's hand.

The rabbit shifter snatched it away and scowled. "I'm still mad at you," he said, once again turning his back on him.

He curled up next to the bed and huffed out a sigh. *Patience.*

Chapter Seven

Rex escorted Aaron to the kitchen and left with Hunter. Big guy seemed like he couldn't ditch him fast enough. Aaron couldn't blame him after being such an emo asshole the night before. The rage that had consumed him had disappeared, replaced by bouts of simmering anger or numbness.

Casey and Mikaela greeted him, and he dutifully took a seat at the table as they bustled about making breakfast. His foot bounced as he glanced around the ultra-modern kitchen, which his entire apartment could fit in.

His thoughts turned to Grandpa Abraham. While a quiet man and not as demonstrative in his affection as *Nonno*, they had been very close. Aaron remembered asking him about the numbers tattooed on his arm. Grandpa Abraham had said, "A reminder I faced evil and survived." The pride and strength ringing through his grandpa's words was almost tangible.

"Food's ready. Come serve yourself."

Caught in long-ago memories, he loaded his

plate in a haze. David was all he had left. Would he ever see his brother again?

He forced himself to start eating as he listened to Casey and Mikaela chat. Those two clearly defaulted to happy. They were damn good cooks, too.

Aaron leaned back in his chair. "That was really good. I feel like I could eat all day."

"Your body's still adjusting to shifting," Casey said before chomping on a piece of bacon.

"Rex told me you used to suppress your wolf. How did you do it?

"I became a vegetarian and had to stay as calm as possible. It wasn't easy. I did it so no one would know about me, but you're safe here. You can shift anytime you want."

"I don't want to be a rabbit ever again."

"I know this is a tough adjustment, but the rabbit is part of you. If you embrace your abilities and accept who you are, it will only make you stronger."

Aaron's fingers thumped on the table.

"Would you like to see what you look like when shifted?" Casey asked.

He nodded. Better get it over with.

Casey held up his phone, displaying an image of Rex snuggling a black-and-white bunny. Was it possible to feel completely freaked out and affectionate all at once? How had the big guy gotten under his skin?

"Want to go for a walk? I'll give you a tour."

"Yeah, that'd be great. I just need to find my shoes." The last time he'd seen them was in the woods. Were they still out there?

"They're by mine."

Aaron followed the small wolf shifter to the

entryway. He stared at the neat row of shoes.

"It's a Minnesota thing. We remove our shoes when we enter a home so we don't track snow and stuff through it. And as shifters, we're pretty much anti-shoe to begin with." Casey grinned and slipped his bare feet into a pair of flip-flops.

"Isn't it too cold to wear those now?" Aaron asked, cramming his socked feet into his sneakers.

"Nah. And when it gets cold, I just wear socks with them."

He must not have masked his horror very well because the other man laughed. "Just kidding. You should have seen your face. You looked just like Hunter when I told him the same thing."

He doubted that.

A weight lifted off Aaron as soon as they were outside. The fresh air and autumn sunshine soothed him.

"Alpha house is at the center of our town." Casey pointed out other houses in the distance as well as the community center, school, stores, and businesses as they walked. It was a regular little town.

"Are all packs set up like this?"

"The big ones are. The Pawlak pack is one of the oldest, largest packs in the country. We provide services to the smaller packs in the Midwest and our Canadian neighbors."

People greeted them as they passed. Although they seemed friendly, they made Aaron twitchy. Maybe the rabbit inside sensed their predators.

"How are you doing?" Casey asked.

Aaron wouldn't fully admit to tweaking out. "Fine, except for the strong urge to munch on that clover."

Casey chuckled.

"How do you keep the feds off your back? Seems like Homeland, or ATF, or whatever would come knocking on your door."

"The Shifter Council is very old and powerful. They provide government funding and have people in key positions. Our communities are left alone."

Aaron's mind raced. Shit, there was a whole crazy world he hadn't known existed. He had new respect for the conspiracy theorists he'd normally thought of as crack pots.

He stopped. "Wait, do aliens exist?"

"You never know who walks among us." Casey grinned.

Aaron's next question about Big Foot was cut off by five teenagers bounding over from the basketball court. They were still in that awkward colt-legged, feet-too-big-for-their-bodies age.

Casey waved to them. "Boys, this is Aaron."

A chorus of "hey, Aarons" came from the kids who quickly introduced themselves. One of them added, "Sorry we chased you, dude. Our wolves are a little wild sometimes." The boy blushed, his bangs flopping into his big puppy eyes. It was tough to be angry when he looked at those earnest, bashful faces.

"No big deal. Just don't do it again."

"Oh, no. Rex'd have our balls for sure," their designated leader said, looking a bit terrified.

"Speaking of which, let's go check out the gym." Casey led the way to the side of the school.

"Nice school. Better than some of the places I attended."

"My dad's good about supporting our community. I'll have big shoes to fill when I'm Alpha one day."

He gave Casey's flip-flops a meaningful glance. "Does that mean you'll grow out of those?"

The small shifter laughed. "Hell no."

Aaron's smile slipped as they entered the gymnasium complete with full basketball court and bleachers. At the far end of the otherwise empty room, Hunter and Rex sparred in what appeared to be Krav Maga on steroids with Brazilian Jiu-Jitsu thrown in. Too bad David wasn't here to see this. Holy shit, they were so strong and fast. The warriors moved in perfect tandem, as if they knew each other's strengths and weaknesses. Intimately.

"They were lovers." His throat burned.

"Yep."

"Aren't you jealous?" Ugly tendrils swirled through him, and Aaron longed for the numbness.

"Nope. Hunter's my mate."

"What's that?"

Casey tugged his shirt away from his neck and shoulder, displaying a scar. "It's like soul mates with teeth. Through our bond, I sense what Hunter is feeling, so no jealousy."

"So, you feel when the other is in pain and stuff?"

"Yeah. Watch." Casey stared at the huge man. His breathing quickened, and his eyes went wolfy. His natural scent's potency strengthened, and Aaron instinctively retreated a few steps from the small wolf shifter.

Hunter's head snapped toward them. He spoke to Rex before stalking the length of the gym. Without stopping, he slung Casey over his massive shoulder and headed for the exit. Casey laughed and called out, "See you later!"

He shook his head. Wolves were such cavemen. Rex sidled up next to him, sweat gleaming on his skin. Aaron had the insane urge to lick him, to see if he tasted as good as he smelled.

"Since Casey took my training buddy, you want to go for a run?" the shifter asked, clearly unaware of his R-rated thoughts. The big guy hesitantly smiled, likely trying to feel out if Aaron was still angry with him.

But he couldn't stay mad at the handsome man who fucking smelled like Christmas and Hanukkah combined.

"Sure." Aaron fought for a casual tone.

Rex's smile broadened, exposing those sexy dimples. *Damn, he is freaking gorgeous.*

They left the school and walked across the little town. Once they came to the gravel road, they started an easy jog. Aaron experienced the same excitement as before when they increased the pace. He took off, legs pumping, feet pounding gravel. He glanced back, stunned at the distance between them. He slowed and turned to jog backward. "What's wrong, old man, can't keep up?"

"Fucker, I'm twenty-eight. Hardly ready for a walker," Rex growled.

Aaron snickered and turned to run forward again.

Soon a large, brown wolf shot past him and stopped several yards ahead. Aaron swore the beast laughed at him.

"Cheater."

He ran with the wolf for a while before collapsing in the grass at the side of the road. His sides heaving, he laughed. Rex's wolf sat at his side, his tongue sticking out of his wolfy smile.

"I never had a dog. Would you play fetch with me?"

The wolf knocked him over and licked his face in response.

"Oh, gross. Stop that." Aaron squealed and giggled.

On the way back, Aaron gathered Rex's clothes, which were littered along a stretch of the road instead of in one pile. He must have stripped while still running, the silly man. Aaron blushed when he gingerly handled his underwear, picturing them hugging Rex's fabulous ass.

The wolf made a snorty sound.

"Oh, shut up."

Chapter Eight

"**R**ex, how are you searching for David?"

"Let me show you my lair," the wolf shifter said in faux creepy voice and waggled his eyebrows before leading the way to the basement, which looked straight out of a cop show. One wall had a bulletin board with pictures, notes, and lines drawn on it. A bank of monitors and computers covered every available space on a table. Each had different data and camera feeds.

"Den Mother extracted some images from your memories. We have a few of The Brotherhood identified." Rex pointed to their pictures and named them. "We're running through their backgrounds, including known locations and associates. It takes time. They've split up by now. I think David is with the muscle."

"They could be anywhere. Europe for all we know." The enormity of it overwhelmed Aaron.

The large man shook his head. "They're still in the US. Den Mother's got eyes and ears on all major transportation out of the States."

"How did you get access to all these cameras?

And here, are those satellite images?"

"Akio's organization has a long reach."

"Is this legal?"

"Nope. Not going to find these guys following the law." The big guy studied the monitor before typing furiously on the keyboard.

"That's not Google."

"Google doesn't work where I'm hunting. This is the Dark Web."

"Shit, I thought that was only urban legend."

"It's very real. You want to find scary, illegal shit, it's here." Rex concentrated on his task, his fingers typing a mile a minute, while the tip of his tongue stuck out the corner of his mouth. *Fuck that's adorable.*

"So, this is what you did for Akio?"

"Yep, I was one of his best trackers."

"He said you'd kill for me. What did he mean?"

"I'm an assassin. Well, mostly retired now. Den Mother pulled us in to help."

"You and Hunter." The two were like superheroes among mere mortals. Those mere mortals being werewolves.

"Yep. He's a master assassin. Never misses his target. Can fucking shoot the wings off a fly." Rex chuckled. "Good thing he figured out Casey was his mate."

"What do you mean?"

"Casey was our last assignment."

"Who'd want to kill him?" Aaron gulped, shocked someone would harm the gentle shifter.

"Pawlak's beta had delusions of grandeur and wanted Casey gone so he'd become Alpha one day. We fucked up his plans."

"Where is this beta now?" *Did shifters have prisons?*

"Dead." Rex's expression and tone were flat, his eyes hard.

A zing of energy coursed through him. Lethal Rex was sexy.

"How did Hunter know they were mates?"

"Scent. Mates emit hormones that are the best scents the other has smelled, often associated with memories. And there's the insane attraction." Rex avoided looking at him.

"Oh, here, this is for you." The wolf shifter handed him an iPod.

Aaron automatically went to the music library. It contained all the music he'd downloaded on his phone. He had music. His feet bounced in excitement. "How did you do this?"

"Easy, just hacked your account and loaded the new device. By the way, using your birthdate as a password isn't very secure."

Rex returned to the viewing the screen.

"I want to help. What can I do?"

"How about you monitor those feeds for alerts. I've got facial recognition algorithms programmed for those four." The large man pointed out their pictures. "Tell me if an alert message pops up."

Aaron's cheeks flushed, ashamed he'd underestimated the big guy's intelligence. Just because Rex was a musclebound god didn't mean he was dumb.

He listened to music as they worked side by side, close enough for their legs or shoulders to occasionally brush, innocent touches setting Aaron on fire. He surreptitiously reached down and adjusted himself.

Rex cleared his throat. "I need a break. Let's go work out and then get dinner."

He couldn't believe the shifter was hungry after the bag of Doritos, Slim Jims, and everything else he'd consumed since lunch. Dude ate like a teenager.

Rex launched a video chat window, and a handsome blond man who could have been Paul Walker's clone appeared on the screen. Were good looks an assassin job requirement?

"Hey, Garrett, ready to spot me, man?"

"Sure. Who's your wingman?"

"This is Aaron. We're looking for his brother, David."

"Well, hello, Aaron. I have a question for you. Is your brother as cute as you?"

"We're identical twins."

"Hot damn, let's find this dude."

Aaron laughed as Rex signed off. "Is everyone in your group gay?"

"Yes. Shifters aren't very tolerant in general, so we tend to flock together."

Chapter Nine

In the gym, Rex showed him how to kick properly then held a large, black pad. Aaron half-heartedly kicked it a few times. This was more David's thing. The big guy didn't look impressed.

"This would be better with music." Rex dropped the pad and trotted to the wall. A familiar rock anthem flooded the gym.

"'Eye of the Tiger,' really?" He smirked as the wolf shifter jogged back and picked up the pad.

"You needed inspiration. Now, stop thinking like a human and kick the shit out of me."

"That's easy for you to say. You're a badass wolf. I'm a fucking bunny."

"And such a cute little rabbit, too, with that fluffy white tail of yours."

Aaron glared without much heat. "Perv, checking out my bunny ass."

"You know it."

He kicked the pad, putting all his muscle into it. Rex toppled over and skidded five feet across the floor.

"Holy shit! Are you okay?"

He dropped to his knees by the shifter when he didn't respond. Rex's eyes were closed. Aaron felt for a pulse. Good, he hadn't killed him, at least. He gingerly touched the wolf shifter's head, feeling for a lump before moving to his torso. Rex groaned, his eyelids fluttering.

"Thank fuck, thought I'd killed you."

"Didn't know you cared so much."

Aaron realized his hands still skimmed Rex's body and snatched them away. "Do you need a doctor?"

The large man moaned as he sat up. "Nope, just glad you didn't nail the boys that hard."

They moved on to punching a heavy boxing bag, and then Rex wanted to see how he could get out of holds. They started with Rex grasping him from behind. Aaron became hyperaware of the powerful body pressed close, his scent swirling around him. He tried to follow the wolf shifter's instructions, but his brain remained in a lust-induced fog. Rex did a move that had him on his back on the mat, the large man's body covering his. *Fuck.* Aaron bit his lip, stifling a groan.

"Damn, you're fucking heavy. What did you eat for lunch, a moose?" he snarked, desperate to quell his raging hormones.

"Are you calling me fat? That hurts my feelings, man."

"Ha, you don't have feelings."

"Think not?" Rex's eyes shimmered with heat, and Aaron felt a bulge against his thigh.

The wolf shifter nuzzled against the side of Aaron's jaw, his lips trailing up to whisper over his mouth. He moaned, letting Rex's tongue dance with his. He rubbed against the strong shifter, the ache inside him intense. He needed.... What was he doing? His brother was out there with some seriously sick fucks, while he made out with Mr. Hot Stuff.

He ripped his mouth from Rex's and shoved at his chest. To his credit, the other man quickly lifted his weight off him and sat back on the mat, resting his head on his knees as he caught his breath.

Aaron wiped his mouth with a trembling hand. Fuck, he needed to get his shit together. "Was this a ploy to seduce me?" he sneered, sitting up.

The large man glowered at him. "You can't deny the chemistry between us."

"Right, big, handsome shifter. I should just give you my ass." Strange how verbally sparring with Rex made him feel...alive.

"You and I...we are the same."

Aaron made a show of looking him up and down. "Oh, yeah, just like twins." He winced, thinking of David.

The wolf shifter shook his head. "We don't trust easily, and we both use our mouths to push people away."

"So, why don't you get the message?"

"Because your mouth is saying one thing while your body is saying another."

"You don't know anything."

"I can smell your arousal, see your skin flush, hear your heart beat faster, and your voice...." Rex's eyes flashed golden fire.

He didn't know about his voice, but Rex's flowed over him like melted chocolate. "What about my voice?"

"It gets deeper, and the Italian New Yorker comes out from hiding. You front like you don't care, but the truth is you care too much. You've got all these walls. Might miss something special if you don't let anyone in."

Aaron bristled. "Yeah, because you're an open book. Where's your background file?"

"I don't have one. When I took the job, my entire identity was erased, and I became a ghost. But I will answer anything you ask me."

He asked the one question he figured Rex wouldn't answer. "How did you become an assassin?"

Ah, Aaron had to start with the most difficult question of all. Rex set his face in a neutral mask as his past swirled to the surface.

"Only Den Mother knows this." He paused, words like rusty nails in his throat. "I came from a small pack in Southern California made up of old people, women, and children. The last that remained from a pack war. We were poor and had next to nothing. I worked three jobs so we'd have food. One day I came home late after taking an extra shift. Everyone was dead. Slaughtered. Sweet, innocent people who wouldn't hurt anyone."

Aaron's mouth hung open. "What? Why?"

"A coyote shifter wanted the land, so he took it. He planned to build tunnels into Mexico so he could run drugs and guns. I went into the desert, tracked each and every one of his cartel members down, and killed them. But his personal bodyguards captured me breaking into his house. I was prepared to die. So young and stupid, I hadn't anticipated the torture...."

Rex rubbed a thumb across the cheekbone that had been shattered and healed long ago. He winced at the sympathy in his mate's eyes.

"Did he...?" Aaron paused like the word *rape* was too horrible a word to say.

"Yeah, but after a few days, he lost interest and tossed me out into the desert to die. Fucker wrapped me in silver chains so I couldn't shift. I lay there ready to join my pack when a dark figure appeared out of nowhere. I thought I was hallucinating. I asked 'Are you death?' He replied 'No, but I bring it to those who deserve it most.' I waited for him to kill me. Instead, Akio cared for me until I healed then he offered me a job. I learned all types of fighting, weapons, and refined my natural tracking abilities. My first assignment, I put a bullet in that fucking drug lord's brain."

"How old were you?"

"Fifteen."

Aaron grasped his hand. Rex stared at their joined hands. Aaron's olive skin tone was lighter than his own, and while he had thick, blunt fingers, his mate's were long and elegant. Sparks of energy spread up his arm before the rabbit shifter released him.

Not knowing what to do with the loss, he fisted his hand and rolled his knuckles into the mat. "How did you become a musician?"

His mate smiled. "I was surrounded by music from birth. My mom was an amazing singer and taught me to play piano when I was three. I loved listening to my *nonno* play his violin. I begged him to teach me. I learned on a smaller instrument, until I grew enough to play his. It was a handcrafted antique with the most beautiful, rich sound. I've played Strads worth millions but nothing compared to that violin. *Nonno* gave it to me during my bar mitzvah. Told me he was proud of the man I'd become." The rabbit shifter's smile was bittersweet.

"Where is it?" Rex would make sure his mate had his violin.

"Destroyed." Aaron frowned and clenched his fists.

Would he shift again? Rex ran his hand over his mate's arm. Aaron flinched and gazed at him in surprise like he'd forgotten his presence. His mate didn't shift, thank fuck, but took a deep breath and continued.

"David and I were often separated in foster care. I got really good at sneaking out to check on him. Finally, we were placed together. It seemed like a nice place. The lady was sweet, but turned out she was addicted to prescription meds and often too out of it to take care of us. To protect us."

Rex ground his molars, dread filling him.

"See the man of the house liked to knock us around. He'd look for any excuse to do so, and, soon, there didn't even need to be a reason. I didn't like the way he watched David, so I drew the attention to me. One day, the bastard screamed at me for scratching his precious car. I hadn't even touched it. He said he'd bust my ass just like he'd busted my violin. I went ape-shit and hit him." Aaron shook his head. "I know now I'd played right into his hands. He'd wanted me to fight. He started punching and kicking me. I was so scared. He grabbed me around the throat, choking me. I knew I was going to die. Then he made this odd sound and released me, clutching his back. David had stabbed him.

"I had to protect my brother, so I told the police I had done it. They wouldn't listen when we told them it was self-defense. Who would believe two orphans instead of an upstanding member of society who had a team of lawyers and a judge or two in his pocket?

"David moved to a really good home, and I spent two years in kiddie prison. They had a music program there. The violin was a piece of junk, but it was something to play. If it hadn't been for that program, I'm not sure I would have made it. I spent the rest of my teen years in a halfway house. When I turned eighteen, my record was sealed, and I applied to Juilliard with a borrowed instrument."

Rex swallowed the blood that filled his mouth as a result of biting the inside of his cheek raw. He grasped Aaron's shoulder and gently hauled him against his body, hugging his mate close. Sliding his nose into the rabbit shifter's soft hair, he inhaled his scent before kissing the side of his head.

Aaron lurched back. "I don't know why I told you all that. I don't even like you."

Rex knew the words were meant to deflect but still felt the needles of hurt. *Patience.*

"Ouch. Not even a bit?" he asked in his sexiest drawl.

"Maybe a smidge," Aaron groused, and Rex's heart surged.

"Wearing you down." He smirked with a wink. He stood and held out a hand to help the other man up.

His mate rolled his eyes but took his hand.

Chapter Ten

Aaron showered before dinner. He expected Rex to be at the table already, but he was a no show. Instead, he sat next to a noticeably empty chair and half-listened to Mikaela and Casey's discussion. Hunter was head down, digging into his dinner like it was his last. Mrs. H had gone out with friends, and Aleksander had left town for a council meeting.

"Any luck finding a new teacher, Casey?" Mikaela asked.

"Sorry, there aren't a lot of teachers like Ms. Sims. Like art, music's not a priority with shifters."

Music? Aaron's interest increased.

"But look what you've done since you've been here. The kids love the new art curriculum, and a few of the moms are asking if you'd consider teaching adult classes. You could start a music program, too."

"I'd love to, but I'm not qualified to teach music. If only Ms. Sims' mate hadn't been from another pack. She was a real find."

"I'm worried about Ethan. He's been so depressed since she left. I sit with him while he practices, but I can't give him any direction."

"What does he play?" The two glanced at him in surprise.

"Piano."

Aaron's focus had been the violin for years, but he'd still kept up with the piano as a connection to his mom. "What's his skill level?"

"Ah, beginner, I think. He's five," Mikaela said.

"I can help him...while I'm here."

Mikaela's eyes beamed as she smiled. "Wonderful. Do you have time after dinner to meet him?"

Aaron glanced at the empty chair again and shrugged a shoulder. "Sure."

Casey grinned. "Thanks, man."

Mikaela rushed off and by the time he'd finished eating, she'd arranged for them to meet Ethan and his parents at the community center.

Ethan's parents were nice. They couldn't stop saying how grateful they were for him spending time with their son. Their love for the boy was both beautiful and tough for Aaron to see. They patiently sat off to the side as he worked with Ethan, who shyly greeted him but slowly opened up when Aaron had him do warm-up drills.

Ethan had been learning *Für Elise*. Time passed quickly as the boy listened to Aaron's instruction and easily adapted his playing to match.

After promising they would continue the next day, Ethan left with his parents, and Aaron returned to the Alpha house with Mikaela.

"You were really good with him."

"He's a great kid. If anyone's good with people, it's you."

"Thanks. I wanted to go to college so I could become a social worker, but it doesn't look like that's going to happen." Mikaela's eyes welled with tears, and she quickly brushed them away.

Aaron's stride faltered. He'd never seen Mikaela unhappy.

"Why?"

"I got accepted, but Hunter won't let me go. Said it was too dangerous. But it's a shifter school. How much danger would I be in?"

"Want me to talk to him?"

"Nah, you're still on his bad side. You don't need to get in more trouble. I'll figure something out."

He gave her a hug before heading to the basement. Only Hunter monitored the screens.

"Where's Rex?"

"He left. Had some business to take care of."

He sat in his assigned area and shared any alerts with the wolf shifter. While the big guy wasn't mean to him, he certainly wasn't a ray of sunshine either. He missed Rex's easy smile and his flirty, often outrageous comments.

Aaron took a deep breath, shoring up his courage, and turned toward the wolf shifter. "I don't know a lot about your world still. But I hate to see Mikaela miserable because she can't go to college. I also know it's tough being a big brother."

Hunter eyed him. "You and David are twins."

"Yeah, but I'm five minutes older. I would do anything to protect him. It nearly killed me when he joined the Army. I was so afraid he'd get hurt or killed. But it was what he wanted to do, and I knew I had to let him go do his thing." Aaron stared at the large man. "Don't make Mikaela resent you by clipping her wings. Let her fly. Besides, can you image the good she'd do for the pack as a trained social worker?"

Hunter pursed his lips. "I'll think about it."

"Good." Aaron could tell the big wolf shifter was wavering and planned to sic Casey on him later to seal the deal.

It was late when he went upstairs to sleep. Still no Rex. The annoying fucker had shadowed him constantly and now he was just gone. Aaron pushed the disappointment deep inside. Maybe the wolf shifter wasn't into him after all. And what did he care what Rex felt anyway? *Shut up, you're not fooling anyone.*

He heard a scratching sound at the bedroom door. When he opened it, Priss pranced in and hopped onto the bed. Two wolves sat in the hall, one with black fur and other cream with red tints. Hunter and Casey.

"So, we're having a slumber party tonight, huh guys? Well, come on in, and make yourselves comfortable." He glanced at the dog curled in a tiny ball. "Looks like Priss has a head start."

He turned off the lights and navigated to the bed while the two shifters settled, their heads resting on each other's backs. A pang of longing shot through Aaron. His eyes were gritty, and his mind raced. He flopped this way and that but couldn't get comfortable. He must have annoyed Priss who jumped down to join the wolves on the floor.

He heard a huff. Hunter's wolf stood next to the bed. A particularly fragrant dirty shirt of Rex's hanging from his mouth. Embarrassed by his obvious obsession with Rex, he thanked the shifter and accepted the offering. He'd have expected something like this from Casey but not his gruff mate. Aaron settled, snuggling the shirt. In a way, it was like holding the big lunk, and on that thought, he fell asleep.

Chapter Eleven

Rex stared at the naked, struggling piece of shit tied to the chair. It'd been easy to identify the brothers' former foster father, track down the motherfucker, access his house's security code, and find his videos. With just a few keystrokes, he'd found digital evidence Michael Shaw's wife, Jenny, hadn't died from an accidental drug overdose a year after the twins had been removed, along with years' worth of videos showing Michael sexually abusing boys. His wolf thrummed close to the surface ready for violence, ready to avenge the victims.

He unsheathed his knife and held it for the waste of human space to see, knowing it was a scary piece of steel. Michael's eyes widened before he pissed himself. His cries were muffled by the gag in his mouth. Rex approached and placed the knife against the man's throat.

"How does it feel to be completely vulnerable? Just like your wife and all those little boys you hurt. I could kill you right now. Slice through your jugular and be done."

Michael trembled and grunted. His eyes bulged.

Rex slid the knife down the man's sternum and over his bloated stomach, applying enough pressure to shallowly slice his skin. "Or I could gut you and let you bleed out slowly." His hand continued south, and he pressed the sharp point right next to the man's shriveled manhood. "Or maybe I'll cut off this pathetic cock and feed it to you."

Michael bucked, and blood flowed down his thigh from the knife's bite. Rex yanked it back. Stupid fuck would unman himself without him doing a damn thing. After wiping the blade on the arm of the couch, he sheathed his knife.

"But it would be too kind to end your life. I think you need to suffer."

His wolf growled, remembering Aaron's time in juvie. Being locked up was a shifter's worst nightmare.

Rex launched a video on the big screen, and Michael yelled into the gag as footage of him suffocating his wife played. "Thought you'd deleted that, didn't you? I'm sure the police will be very interested in seeing this and all those other files." He pointed to the computer open to the previously hidden partition and the pile of DVDs at the bastard's feet. "Hope you like prison, motherfucker. I hear they give special treatment to child rapists."

He strode to the wall and jabbed the panic button. "Help, there's an intruder in the house!" Rex yelled in a perfect imitation of Michael's voice. The asshole stared at him, his eyes blinking in astonished surprise. *Yeah, I have all kinds of skills.*

Rex exited the house and returned to his rental. Damn, the Benz was sweet. Maybe he should get one.

He drove until he came to a closed campground. Getting out of the car, he removed the disc labeled "David" from of his jacket pocket and threw it in a fire pit. Lighting it on fire, he wished he could burn away the images in his brain. He hadn't watched all of it, but he'd seen enough. Pain stabbed through his heart. The brothers were truly identical. He shouldn't have removed evidence, but there was enough to bury the bastard in a supermax prison forever. Unlike Michael, he knew he couldn't delete the videos without destroying the hard drive, but he'd hidden the David files on the computer, in a way only the best hackers could find. Thank fuck it didn't appear Michael had shared them on the net. No one else needed to see them. Aaron's brother had suffered enough.

His phone rang as he watched the disc bend and twist. "Hey, Den Mother."

"You didn't kill him."

Of course Akio monitored his activity in Colorado. He waited for the dressing down. To be told he'd lost his edge.

"I'm proud of you."

"What?"

"I would not have judged had you removed that filth from this world, but you took the higher path. Aaron is a very lucky man to have you as a mate."

The pressure in Rex's chest eased a bit. "Did you find it?" Michael Shaw's finances had confirmed what he'd suspected.

"I've brokered a price. It's going to place a substantial dent in your retirement fund."

"I don't care about the amount. Just do it." He had more money than he knew what to do with any way.

"Consider it done. Bianca will be waiting in Duluth once you land."

"Thanks, Akio." Rex waited until the disc turned to ash before returning to the Benz. He had a mate to get home to.

Chapter Twelve

"It's amazing to see how Ethan responds to Aaron. What a special connection," Mrs. H said.

Rex's steps faltered before he charged into the kitchen.

"Who's Ethan, and what's he been doing with my mate?" He'd eviscerate anyone who touched his rabbit shifter. His wolf snarled.

"Whoa, slow your roll there, caveman. Ethan's five years old," Hunter said.

Rex unclenched his fists as the heat of his fury receded. The time away from his mate had been more difficult than he'd imagined.

"They're in the community center. I'll take you." Casey stood and led the way. "Was your mission successful?"

"Please. I wouldn't be here if it wasn't." He ruffled Casey's hair affectionately.

"Kill anyone?"

"Nope, but made a piece of shit wish I had."

"You're so getting laid."

"Not why I did it. I want to show I listened to

him. Most of all, I want him to be happy. Well, the best he can be, anyway."

"As grand gestures go, this is off the charts."

"Let's hope he thinks so, too,' Rex said when they entered the community center.

They peered into a room that housed a large piano. Mikaela glanced up and smiled before ushering a young boy out. Casey joined her, leaving Rex alone to watch his mate...who turned away to him and began to play the piano. The music was dark, intense, rising with passion. He moved closer when Aaron's head tipped back, his eyes closed as he stroked the keys with long, nimble fingers. God, would he look like that during sex? So. Fucking. Beautiful. *Mine.*

The song came to an end, and Aaron's fingers rested on keys. He inhaled deeply before half turning and spearing Rex with a hot glance.

"You're back." His tone held accusation, while his heated eyes stripped him bare.

Rex's muscles bunched with nervous tension. Going on the defense, he assumed a cocky grin, widened his stance, and hooked his thumbs in his jeans belt loops. "Did you miss me?"

Aggression radiated off his mate as he rose from the piano bench and stalked toward him.

Rex retreated until he rested against the wall, his wolf enjoying this game, even if he was the prey.

Aaron followed him, not stopping until he was up close and personal. Slamming his hands on the wall on either side of Rex, he caged him in. Rex's cock jerked in response, and his wolf rumbled in approval. Maybe Aaron had a bit of wolf in him after all. He sighed, his mate's tantalizing scent surrounding him.

Home.

"You left."

"Sorry. Had business."

"I don't know what I want to do more, hit you or kiss you."

"If I have any say, I'd go with kissing."

"I've never felt like this. I want to fucking devour you."

Rex moaned. "I'd be down with that."

"What did you do to me? I'm so freaking horny. I even jerked off in the shower, but it didn't help."

"Shifter stamina and drive. You'll just keep going and going." He smirked.

"I will kill you if you call me the Energizer Bunny."

Rex tsked. "Such violence from a little woodland creature."

Aaron rubbed his chin against the side of his head. Rex's smile broadened. The rabbit shifter had marked him with his scent.

"Fucker." Aaron grunted and ran biting kisses along his jaw. One of his hands tangled in Rex's hair and tugged.

He gasped at the delicious mix of pleasure and pain. "Yes, *mi conejito.*"

The other man stared at him. "Did you just call me your little rabbit? Does this feel small to you?" Aaron asked as he ground his cock against him.

"No." Rex stifled a chuckle. His rabbit was fierce. "No slight intended to your manhood, just an endearment...means my bunny."

"Endearment," Aaron spat. "Fucking Alpha asshole."

"Actually, I'm a beta."

"Whatever. You're a pushy, arrogant man who drives me crazy."

"I prefer to think I'm confident."

"Just because you're a big bad wolf doesn't automatically mean you're top dog." Aaron leaned in and nipped his ear.

Rex groaned and tipped his head, giving his mate access to his throat. Aaron pushed all his wolf buttons. "I'm versatile." He gasped.

The rabbit shifter eased back, and Rex moaned at the loss. His mate's hot hazel gaze pierced through him.

"So, if I told you I wanted you to suck my dick, what would you do?"

Rex gulped in air; the need to satisfy his mate consumed him. "I'd drop to my knees and give you my mouth."

Aaron's nostrils flared. "Just like that."

"*Sí*. I'll give you whatever you want...whatever you need."

"And if I want it all?" The rabbit shifter rubbed his hard ridge against him.

Fuck. He could hardly breathe, lust blazing through him as he stared into his mate's eyes. "Then you will have it."

"Let's go to your room."

Chapter Thirteen

As soon as they were in the relative privacy of the Alpha house's second floor hallway, they were in each other's arms, kissing like they'd been separated for weeks. They broke off when oxygen became a need.

"Why are you smiling like that? It's creepy," Aaron said.

"I have a surprise for you," Rex said, taking his hand and tugging him into the bedroom.

Aaron spied the violin case on the bed. When he opened it, he gasped. With trembling fingers, he traced the surface, gingerly brushing the small nick in the wood on the left side. His grandfather's violin. Here. He pulled it out of the case, and examined it, relieved to find the instrument in excellent condition.

"How?" The rest of the words caught in his throat.

"I figured it'd been sold rather than destroyed. I dug around and located the owner."

"It's an antique. Must have cost a fortune." He stared at Rex, stunned.

"In addition to being handsome, I have a

boatload of money. I'm told I'm quite a catch." Rex preened.

Shit, Aaron had no defense against this intoxicating man, but he had to try. "Did you do this to get into my pants?"

"Seemed you were the one trying to get into mine," the big shifter said with a wink.

"I don't know how I can ever repay you."

"Play something for me."

"Any requests?"

"Just not the theme from *Schindler's List*. Makes me cry like a baby."

Aaron sat on the wooden chair while Rex perched on the end of the bed. He considered what he should play as he tuned the violin and rosined the bow. Concentrating on the notes in his head, he played enough of "Eye of the Tiger" for the other man to recognize it.

Rex laughed. "How did you do that without sheet music?

Aaron shrugged. "I have a good ear. This is better with a cello accompanying it but...." He played Metallica's "Nothing Else Matters."

"That was fucking awesome."

Now that he'd warmed up, he gave Rex a taste of Tchaikovsky's "Violin Concerto in D."

"Thank you." Tears welled in Aaron's eyes as the music echoed in his head. The sound was as rich and true as he'd remembered.

Rex stood and took a few steps toward the door.

"Where are you going?"

"Thought you'd like to be alone."

"I want to be with you. That is, if you still want to."

Please. Missed wolf.

"Hell, yes."

Aaron carefully returned the violin to the case and placed it on the floor by the closet. He turned, and Rex sat at the end of bed waiting for him.

He gulped, his earlier bravado leaving him. How could he compete with someone like Hunter or any of Rex's other lovers? For once, he could relate to the timid creature inside.

The shifter reached out and pulled him to stand between his legs. "Hey, it's just you and me here. No one else."

Is the wolf shifter a mind reader?

"I don't have a lot of experience." Music had always been his priority, and he hadn't made time for much else.

"Probably proves I'm a Neanderthal, but that's a major turn-on." The big guy's smile was dazzling.

"Yeah?"

"Mmm-hmm, whatever we do, I know it's going to be awesome. Consider me your personal playground." His eyes flashed gold.

His confidence bolstered, Aaron kissed him. Would he ever get enough of those full, soft lips? His fingers tangled in the wolf shifter's thick hair, and he hummed against his lips. While Rex fully participated, he'd kept his hands on the bed. Aaron yanked the shifter's shirt over his head and caressed his shoulders and down one muscular arm. He traced ropy veins on Rex's forearm and large hand. Talk about vein porn. Aaron had always had a thing for hands, and the big guy's were awesome. Holding one up to his face, he traced one of the veins with his lips before capturing one of Rex's thick fingers in his mouth and sucking on it. Damn, he tasted good.

Rex moaned. Aaron released his finger with a "pop" and let go of his hand. The wolf shifter returned it to the mattress. Aaron massaged his firm pecs. Heartened by Rex's groans, he dropped to his knees and licked and nipped his pebbled nipples.

He pushed the shifter back on the bed, his lips moving along Rex's amazing abs before his tongue traveled all the dips and valleys. Hard as a rock, and his heart beating wildly with anticipation, he unfastened Rex's jeans and yanked them off. The briefs strained to conceal Rex's monster erection. He pressed his face against the cloth and inhaled. Pure heaven.

"You smell so good."

"What do I smell like, *conejito*?"

He let the bunny comment go since he kind of liked Rex saying it. "Like peppermint, pine trees, and my *bubbe's* potato latkes."

Rex's lips twisted into a little grin.

"What do I smell like to you?" Aaron held his breath.

"Like my **mamá's** cinnamon churros, vanilla, and the ocean."

Could they be mates? He'd certainly come to care for the lunkhead.

He's the one. The one for us.

"Seems like one of us is overdressed," Rex said with a smile.

Aaron stripped down to his underwear and covered the shifter with his body, the skin-to-skin contact causing them both to moan. They kissed for several minutes while rubbing their clothed cocks together. Dry humping had never been so erotic, so damn good.

Aaron slid down Rex's body and nuzzled against him again before easing his briefs off. After licking the tip, he took in as much as he could, bobbing and sucking. Thankfully Rex remained still, because he couldn't handle the big guy pumping. His mouth slipped, and he gagged, taking in too much. Tears sprang in his eyes. Aaron's cheeks heated in embarrassment.

"It's okay. You're amazing. Helps to use your hand and don't worry about taking it all. Feels so good."

He resumed sucking while his hand pumped. He must have been doing something right because Rex murmured in Spanish. Damn, he loved to see the big guy losing control, all because of him.

"Aaron, I want you inside me."

He kissed the tip of Rex's cock before glancing up. "Stuff?"

Rex reached in the nightstand's drawer and handed him a bottle of lube.

"No condom?"

"Beauty of shifter sex. We don't get diseases, including STDs." The big guy smiled.

Aaron sucked in a breath. "I've never barebacked."

"So I'm your first," the large man purred, a gleam in his eyes.

And only whispered through his head.

"But what about pregnancy?"

Rex leaned back on his elbows, his face inscrutable as he eyed Aaron. "I don't know whether to be insulted or intrigued by that question."

Aaron flushed. "My friend Lexie reads a lot of

gay paranormal romances. She told me about a story where male shifters get pregnant. Is that true?"

The big shifter's eyes twinkled, and he shook his head. "Just like humans, we aren't equipped for babies. So none of your *bambinos* will spoil my impressive figure."

Yes, it was an absurd question, but hell he hadn't known it was possible for people to turn into animals until a few days ago. "You must think I'm stupid," Aaron groaned.

Rex's expression turned serious. "No, I think you're amazing. Your world has been turned upside down, and you're still trying to be responsible. That's very sexy. Now come fuck me."

He didn't need to be told twice. "Roll over. I haven't had a chance to explore my entire playground yet."

Rex grinned before he turned. Aaron's hands roamed over Rex's spectacular back and slid his erection along the crack of his ass. Rex moaned and humped against the mattress.

He moved off the big shifter. "Up on your knees."

After Rex complied with a groan, Aaron massaged his hard ass. Damn, the shifter was gorgeous everywhere. Following an urge, he slapped one butt cheek and stilled. *Too kinky?*

Rex hissed in pleasure. "Yes. Do it again."

Aaron grinned. *Oh, yeah.* He swatted the other cheek, Rex's response ratcheting up his own pleasure. He spanked him a few more times until Rex's delicious caramel skin turned a rosy hue. He blew the heated skin before placing a chaste kiss on the top of each cheek. Rex made a gurgling sound.

Aaron's hand trembled as he rubbed his fingers

together, warming the lube he'd squirted on them. He stroked the outside of Rex's hole before breaching it with one finger, starting with only to the first knuckle, and then further in. He listened to the shifter's cues and added a second finger and then another. It was so hot watching the big guy fuck himself on his fingers, moaning for more.

Rex groaned when he removed fingers. Aaron swatted his butt again before pressing his dick to his quivering hole. "I'm going to fuck you now."

He pressed while Rex relaxed and pushed back. They both groaned when the head popped in. He slowly inched forward until his hips rested against Rex's hot ass.

Aaron stopped, struggling for control before he came. Rex's channel clutched tight around him. Without latex, he could feel everything.

"Move. Please."

Aaron began an easy glide, pulling almost all the way out before driving back in again. Encouraged by the sounds Rex made, he thrust in with short, deep jabs. *So good.*

"Yes, fuck me. Fuck me hard."

Leaning forward, Aaron tugged Rex's hair to turn his head. They shared a dirty kiss before Aaron released him.

He pounded into the large man, one hand gripping his hip, the other reaching down and grasping his leaking cock. Aaron jerked Rex's dick in time with his thrusts.

Rex yelled, his warm cum overflowing Aaron's fist. Aaron's eyes crossed as his lover's channel clamped around him, and he came with a groan.

Chapter Fourteen

Several hours later, Rex lay there completely fucked out, floating on a cloud. Aaron snuggled against him with a contented sigh, his need finally sated. Rex's ass ached in the best way possible. Yeah, he was versatile, but it'd been over a year since he'd bottomed. And damn, it'd been worth the wait. If sex was always going to be like this with his rabbit shifter, Rex needed to step up his game and be better prepared, like eating his Wheaties and maybe do some stretching beforehand. He stroked his mate's hair.

"I love your hair. It's so soft."

Aaron grunted. "I look like a cow."

"Could have been worse."

"How?"

"Could've been a guinea pig. You know the calico-colored ones with the crazy cowlicks?"

Heat zigged through him when his mate pinched his nipple.

"Too soon?" Rex quipped.

"You're good at that." Aaron chuckled.

"Pissing you off?"

"Making me laugh."

"I honestly think you're perfect just the way you are."

Aaron stroked his chest. "While I'm not wild about my hair, I do have one thing to thank those bastards for."

"What?"

"My dick's bigger."

Rex let out a surprised sound, half snort, half chuckle.

"It's true. It's thicker and an inch longer."

"Well, then I will need to thank them, too." *Before I kill them.*

Aaron's hand ghosted over his stomach, rubbing in little circles.

"Still can't compete with yours though. What a monster."

"It's not the size that counts but what you do with it. Let's just say I'm very pleased."

Rex felt Aaron's lips tugging into smile against his skin before his mate leaned up, his hand resting on his stomach. His mate's hazel eyes were large. "I've never…. I'm not sure you'll fit."

Rex's wolf howled in primal satisfaction knowing no one had been with his mate *there*.

"It's okay. You don't have to do anything you don't want to."

Aaron bit his lip. "What if I want to try sometime?"

Rex swore his half-comatose dick whimpered as he thought about taking Aaron's sweet virgin ass. He squinted and took a steadying breath.

"When you're ready, you let me know." Rex struggled around the lump in his throat. *Go for casual.* "I'm starving. How about we shower and get this show on the road?"

"Okay, do you want to go first?"

Actually he'd wanted to share but a little space couldn't hurt. "How about you first?"

Rex admired his mate's slender body as he rose. Something red peeked out from under the sheet. He snagged it. How had one of his dirty shirts ended up here? He glanced at his mate and chuckled at the beautiful blush that spread across his man's cheeks as he scurried off to the bathroom.

Chapter Fifteen

Rex stretched his arms over his head and sighed. Thank fuck he'd purchased a superior ergonomic office chair, because he practically lived in it. They'd finally caught a break after getting a visual on one of The Brotherhood's goons in California. Unfortunately, the trail had gone cold, so now he spent more time in this chair than his own bed where he could be curled up with his mate. Aaron tended to sprawl on him, a long leg hooked over his. Rex had gone from never sleeping with anyone to loving being the little spoon.

His mate stayed with him most of the time, which made this hunt tolerable. He glanced at Aaron, sitting next to him listening to music. Soon, he'd be reunited with his brother and all would be right in their world. Rex launched a video chat window to get Garrett's report. As he suspected, his teammate didn't have any good news to share. He rubbed his eyes in frustration and then flailed in his chair when a jet of warm air blew on his crotch.

"Ugh!"

"You okay, man?" Garrett asked, his brow

bunching in concern.

"Yeah, just a leg cramp." Rex fought for a normal tone as his mate mouthed his dick through his shorts. *Fuck.*

The other man chuckled. "That's what happens when you get frisky on a regular basis, you old dog. Where's your better-looking half anyway?"

"Oh, he's umm...around," Rex groaned while his evil mate chuckled against him.

"Hope you have better luck on your shift."

"Thanks." Rex closed the program and tilted his head so he could meet the mischievous eyes under the table.

"What are you doing, babe?"

"Seemed like you needed a morale boost."

"Oh, my morale is *way* up now."

"Oh, I think it can be even better."

"Yeah?"

Aaron nodded and tugged his shorts. Rex lifted his hips and his mate jerked his underwear and shorts down. He sighed when Aaron licked him like an ice cream cone before taking him in his mouth. His mate's eyes sparkled as he continued his sensual assault. His head bobbed, taking in as much as he could, while fisting the rest.

Rex's balls drew up and his toes curled. "Aaron...."

The rabbit shifter didn't back off, but hollowed his cheeks while he sucked. Rex yelled as he came down his mate's throat. He slumped in the chair while Aaron crawled out from under the table, licking his lips.

"Come here," Rex helped him to his feet and kissed him. "Let me return the favor."

Something flashed on one of the monitors, grabbing his attention. "Sorry, I need to look at this."

"What is it?"

"Another sighting in the small town outside of Big Bear Lake. This time of year there's lots of empty cabins. Maybe they're holed up in one."

Rex called and reported in. Den Mother came on the line. "I'm sending a helo to you. Be ready with Hunter in thirty."

"Yes, sir," Rex said and ended the call.

"I want to go with you."

Rex shook his head. "Too dangerous."

"Is it because I'm a rabbit?" Aaron frowned, his hazel eyes darkening.

"It has nothing to do with you being a rabbit. You're not trained for this. Trust me. I'll bring David home."

Aaron sat on the bed with his heart in his throat as Rex got ready. The big guy wore black military attire with twin knives sheathed across his torso and a pistol strapped to his thigh. Damn, he looked like one of those sexy vampire warriors his friend Lexie liked to read about. The ones so badass they had extra letters in their names.

"Stop looking at me like that, or I'm not going to be able to go." Rex gave him a hard kiss.

He blushed. "Can't help it, you're so hot...so lethal."

"You like?" The wolf shifter preened.

"Wear this again when you come home."

Rex chuckled and kissed his forehead. "I love you."

"I...." Aaron choked on the words, fear seizing him. He'd lost everyone he'd ever loved. Would he lose another?

Rex cupped his face. "Hey, it's going to be okay."

Aaron threw his arms around him and hugged him tight. "Good luck, Rex."

"Manuel."

"Hmmm?"

"When I took the job, I took a new name. My real name is Manuel Reyes."

"Always a king."

Rex grinned. "At least by name."

They kissed, and the wolf shifter released him. "I've got to go."

He followed Rex downstairs and watched the two assassins board the helicopter. Akio sure worked in style. Feeling a hand on his shoulder, he turned to Casey.

"It's never easy to see him go," the little wolf shifter said with a sad smile.

"I'm sorry. Hunter wouldn't be going into a dangerous situation if it weren't for David and me."

"Don't be sorry. I'm glad they can help your brother. Here, this is for you," Casey said, handing him a large envelope.

He opened it. There were papers making him an official member of the Pawlak pack. Then Rex's will, naming Aaron as sole beneficiary of his wealth. His eyes misted.

"I'm such a tool. I couldn't even tell him I love him."

"He knows."

"Yeah?"

"You light up anytime he's around." The wolf

shifter smiled.

So much for keeping things to himself.

"Listen, my dad's friends with the Alpha from Los Angeles, which is a few hours from where the guys are going. He's going to fly us out so we can be there to wait for our men."

"Thank you." Just knowing they'd be in the same state made Aaron feel a little better.

Chapter Sixteen

The teams searched for hours, hunting in the night. Rex drank from his canteen and continued on, Hunter covering his six. They came upon another group of cabins. Rex paused and sniffed. While David wouldn't smell yummy like his brother, they should have a familial component to their scent.

The air was ripe with humans...and there...human similar to Aaron and a trace of rabbit. David.

"They're here."

Hunter called in the closest teams.

"Can you tell which one he's in?"

"Not with the human smell clouding the area. Will need to get closer."

The teams fanned out to cover as they advanced.

"There, the large cabin two up to the right."

They surrounded the building. Garrett and Ryland were at the main entrance, while Rex and Hunter took the deck. The others stationed themselves at each of the windows. Rex concentrated on his breathing as his teammates whispered status updates through their coms.

Ryland gave the go ahead, and Garrett kicked in the front door while Hunter broke through the side door.

Two shots were fired in the front of the house as Ry and Garrett relayed two were down. Rex shot a man in the kitchen, and Hunter took one out at the base of the stairs.

As the calls of "clear" sounded, Rex and Hunter advanced up the stairs and methodically opened the doors. All were empty except one.

David stood in the middle of the room. He assumed a defensive position, his fists raised ready for a fight. Rex knew the brothers were twins, but it still weirded him out just how alike they were even with David's buzzed-cut hair.

"Who are you?" David's eyes flashed with defiance.

"We're the good guys. We have Aaron in a safe location."

"You have my brother?"

"Yes, we don't have time to talk, let's go."

"Why should I trust you?"

Rex resisted the urge to roll his eyes. Apparently, the brothers shared the stubbornness trait, as well.

"I know about his grandpa's violin. How special it was to him."

David stared at him. "He told you about the violin? He hasn't talked about it in years."

Garrett's voice sounded in his ear. "We need to retreat."

"Look, I promised him I'd bring you home. So how about we get out of here?"

"Okay. Let's go."

Thank fuck.

"How many men have you seen?" Rex asked as they left the room.

"Four."

Hunter nodded. "Matches the body count."

They would follow rescue protocol, remaining vigilant in case more baddies were unaccounted for. Exiting the cabin, they headed into the woods. Halfway to the extraction point, a laser sight's red dot appeared on David.

"Gun!" Rex tackled the rabbit shifter as Hunter fired. The grunt and the heavy thud of a body falling confirmed his friend had nailed the bastard.

"Thanks, man. Shit, you're bleeding," David said when he helped him off the ground.

"No biggie. Just my shoulder," he replied. Then the world tipped sideways.

"Rex." Hunter held him up.

"Silver...."

***

Aaron and Casey paced in the hospital lobby. The antiseptic smell turned Aaron's stomach. He'd spent a lot of time in hospitals with his childhood injuries and his grandparents' illnesses, and unease filled him just being in one. And now he waited, his dread increasing with each passing minute. Eventually, Hunter ambled down the hall, blood soaking his shirt.

"Hunter, I sensed your pain. Where were you hit?" Casey ran to his mate and grasped his arm.

"Not my blood."

Aaron didn't need the mate bond to sense the

pain and fear radiating off the large shifter. His knees sagged. "Rex?"

Hunter nodded. "He was shot in the shoulder, which normally isn't an issue, but the bullet was specially crafted to harm shifters. Hard shell with tiny silver pellets inside. The pellets spread through his system, and he went into cardiac arrest. Thank God they were able to stabilize him. He's in surgery now."

Aaron felt the tingling sensation signaling changing form. He pleaded to the animal within, *No, please. Let me help our mate.* The sensation passed, and he sighed in relief.

"Is there anything I can do?"

Just then a female nurse appeared. "He's lost a lot of blood. We'll need a donor."

"I don't know his blood type, but I'm his mate."

The nurse looked confused. "But he's male...and isn't marked."

Hunter answered for him, "Yes, it's possible for males to mate, and they're mates even though they haven't claimed each other yet."

The nurse quickly lost the confused look. "Very good. Mate's blood is the best thing for him."

In a daze, Aaron went through the process of giving blood while Hunter told him David was doing well besides being dehydrated. He was receiving fluids and was under observation as a precaution.

With Rex expected to be in surgery for hours, Aaron went to see his brother. David's hair had been shaved close to the scalp, but otherwise, he appeared the same. They hugged. "I'm so glad they found you," Aaron said.

"I'm sorry. You wouldn't have been in this mess

if it weren't for me." David touched Aaron's hair.

He blinked away tears. "Not your fault. Plus, it hasn't all been bad. I found a man willing to put up with my stubborn ass."

"Rex?" David's eyes brightened.

He nodded.

"He took a bullet for me. Didn't even hesitate." His brother squeezed his hand.

Aaron's chest constricted. He couldn't lose him.

Soon, the nurse shooed him out, saying David needed his sleep. Chewing his fingernails to the quick, Aaron paced the hall with Casey and Hunter. He'd memorized the tile pattern on the floor by the time the doctor came out to deliver the news.

He'd almost kissed the surgeon when he told him Rex had pulled though after they'd extracted all the silver beads and given him Aaron's blood.

"I don't think he would have lived without it. Mate's blood has almost magical properties."

Casey hugged him before he entered his mate's room.

Rex's pale skin had a greenish cast as he lay in the hospital bed connected to all kinds of machines. Thick bandages and gauze covered his torso. Aaron's lips quivered. They'd had to crack his chest open to extract all the beads and repair the damage to his heart.

He sat next to the bed, and for the next three days he rarely left.

Once his brother was cleared medically, he'd left the hospital to stay at the L.A. Alpha's house, but he stopped in a few times each day to check on Aaron. Hunter and Casey were also there, camping out in the waiting room. No way in hell the hospital staff would dare tell them to leave.

It was the middle of the night, but Aaron couldn't sleep. Without his brother or friends' reassuring presence, fear loomed large. Would he lose his mate? He clasped Rex's hand and kissed it. His eyes filled with tears. "I love you, you big lunk. You need to get better so you can stick that big, fat cock in my ass and claim me as your mate. Do you hear me?"

"Suddenly feeling the will to live," came a scratchy voice.

"Rex!" He hugged his mate hard enough for him to grunt. "Sorry. I've been so worried." He pressed the nurse's button.

"Is your brother okay?" Rex reached up to brush the tears from his face.

"Yes, he's staying with a local Alpha along with Casey and Hunter. Although they've been here most of the time with me."

"Good friends."

"The best."

Aaron stepped out in the hall at the duty nurse's insistence. He hugged Hunter and Casey. "He's awake."

"Good. We need to get you into a shower stat, dude. You reek," Hunter grumbled.

Casey and Aaron laughed.

Chapter Seventeen

A few days later, Aaron and David visited in the hospital cafeteria.

"How's Rex doing?"

"He's getting better, thank goodness. He's a horrible patient. The nurses run when he starts crabbing. The doctor says we can go home in a few days. I can't wait for you to see Minnesota."

David stared at his coffee cup, while his leg bounced under the table. "About that. I'd love to visit, but I can't live with you."

Aaron's heart skipped. "Where would you go?"

"I met Den Mother this morning. He offered me a job." David paused, running his finger around the rim of the cup. "The Brotherhood is still out there. I'd like to help take them down."

"You'd be putting yourself in danger every time you go out." Aaron's eyes pricked, the fear of losing Rex still fresh. Now David would be in harm's way. "What if they capture you again?"

"There's something about Akio. My gut's telling me I can trust him. I worked out with some of the guys before I came here. It's the first time I've felt like

I belonged since the Army."

He'd just found his brother, and he planned to leave again. But this wasn't about him. He needed to be happy David had found a place, too. He swiped at the tears threatening to spill over.

David gazed at him with troubled eyes. "I hope you don't think I'm a total dick for ditching you."

"Oh, no it's great, David, or do you have a new name now?"

His brother smiled. "I'm still considering."

***

"I hear you've been terrorizing the hospital staff."

Rex glanced up from the latest issue of *Guns & Ammo* to see Akio standing by the door. He grinned at the vampire. "Hey, Den Mother. What are you doing here?"

"I came to drop off your check."

"I didn't expect to be paid. I'd do anything for my mate."

Den Mother nodded. "Yes, I know, but you did important work for the organization."

Rex opened the envelope and looked at the amount, easily triple his usual pay. Enough to remove that dent in his retirement fund. He raised an eyebrow.

"Hazard pay and a thank you."

"For what?"

Den Mother touched the teddy bear on the table. "I loved Erik with all my heart, but he wasn't my mate." Akio met his eyes. "I never thought I would love again...but David...he is my mate."

"Whoa, congrats."

"I'm not sure how to proceed. He has been through so much."

Michael Shaw's chances of survival will be zero once Akio accesses David's memories. His wolf rumbled in agreement.

"A wise man once told me patience is important."

Den Mother smiled. "Thank you, Rex. Enjoy your retirement."

"Count on it."

Chapter Eighteen

Aleksander met them at the door. Rex and Aaron paused to take off their shoes. It felt right placing his next to the big guy's. They were home.

Hunter cruised by with Casey thrown over his shoulder. "Hi, Dad. Bye, Dad. Save us some cake," the small shifter hollered while the big man carried him upstairs.

"We'll talk later, son." The Alpha chuckled, surprising Aaron. "Even I know better than to get between bonded mates. Rex, how are you doing?"

"Fully recovered, sir. Thanks."

"Good. Our pack needs its future beta here and healthy. And, Aaron, how is your brother?"

"He's doing well. He took a job with Akio's group, but hopefully he'll be here to visit during the holidays."

"Excellent. He's always welcome."

They entered the family room and there were balloons, banners, and cake. Mrs. H, Mikaela, Ethan, and his parents were there. After a few hours, Aaron totally envied Hunter's and Casey's alone time. He squeezed Rex's hand and gave him a hopeful look.

"Thanks so much, everyone. I think I'm ready to retire for the night. Aaron?"

"Thank you. See you tomorrow, Ethan, at nine sharp."

Once they were in their room, they were in each other's arms, their mouths connecting with hot and desperate need. A shiver ran through him as the shifter's large hands stroked his back. With a gasp, he released Rex's mouth and buried his face against his mate's neck. The strong pulse reminded Aaron that Rex was safe and alive. He yanked Rex's T-shirt off and caressed his completely healed chest. Not even a scar to show the injury and surgery he'd endured.

He noticed Rex was letting him call the shots as he'd done in the past. "Don't you want to lead?"

"Wasn't sure you were ready for that."

Aaron stripped off his clothes and sprawled out on the bed. "Think of my body as your playground."

Rex cocked his head. "Really?"

"Yep. I meant what I said at the hospital, so get your ass over here and claim me already," Aaron said, deliberately laying the New Yorker accent on thick.

"I love it when you get bossy."

Rex stretched out next to him, and they shared long, deep kisses. Aaron wasn't as disciplined as his mate had been; his hands caressed the large shifter instead of keeping them to himself. The large man didn't seem to mind.

The big guy stroked his hair and broke off to peer into his eyes. "I'm so sorry what happened to you, but I thank God every day you're with me."

Tears pricked his eyes. Damn Rex for being so damn heartfelt and mushy. "I love you."

And he did, he loved the warrior, the computer brain, the smartass, the mushy guy, the killer, and the protector. He loved all the sides that made up this incredible man.

Rex sucked in a breath. "I felt that here," he said, placing a large hand to his own heart. "But how is that possible? We haven't claimed each other yet."

"Maybe having my blood inside you is like a claim."

The big shifter hummed as he nuzzled against Aaron's jaw. "Love you, too, *conejito*."

He sighed while Rex worked his magic, exploring his body with his mouth and hands like he was all that. He didn't fully understand why the large man was so into him. He wasn't anything special. Slender, bordering on scrawny if it weren't for the new muscle definition from his workouts with Rex.

"You're perfect," the big shifter said.

Aaron flushed. This connection thing was going to take some getting used to.

Rex tried to guide him on his stomach. "It's easier this way the first time."

He shook his head. "I want...I need to see your face."

The large man smiled and slipped a pillow under his hips. Aaron had never felt so exposed, but his shyness disappeared as soon as Rex's mouth engulfed his dick. "Oh!"

Rex made him feel so good. As he climbed to orgasm, his mate moved to suck his balls. Aaron thought he would go crazy with lust until Rex did something new. He tongued his sensitive hole. "Fuck! Do that again."

The big shifter chuckled and continued, jacking

him while he did so. Soon Aaron writhed against the sheets. "Please, please, Rex. Love me."

"Oh, babe. What you do to me."

Rex's slick finger stretched him until he could take another. When the big guy found his prostrate, Aaron moaned, pre-cum glistening on his cock.

"Now, please. Need you. Inside."

Rex rose onto his knees, positioned his erection against him, and pressed forward. Aaron did his best to relax. They both sighed when the head popped in.

Rex locked eyes with him, as he began short, gentle thrusts. Aaron wrapped his legs around him and the large shifter snapped his hips with more force.

"Yes," Aaron hissed.

The large shifter drove into him, and he knew he was close. Rex leaned up to kiss him, sloppy and deep, before sinking his teeth where his neck and shoulder met.

Stars bursting in his head, Aaron shouted out as he and Rex came together.

A wave of love and happiness filled Aaron. An amplification of his own feelings. "Holy shit. Did you feel that?"

"Yes, but you still need to make an honest mate out me and bite me."

"We'll have to fix that soon."

Rex was on top of the world. He'd claimed his mate. Now, he was enjoying being the little spoon again while his mate slept. Aaron snuggled against him, and Rex could feel his heart beat and his erection prodding him. He smiled. Someone was waking up.

He sighed when Aaron kissed his shoulder and caressed his chest and stomach, while rubbing his dick against him. Damn, his man had skills.

"Lube?"

Rex handed it to him.

Aaron moved back and prepared him. He loved how his mate patiently worked him, enhancing his pleasure.

"I'm ready."

His mate's cock slid against him again, this time taking him.

"Yes."

They found a rhythm that was so damn good, Rex knew he wouldn't last long.

"Aaron, bite me."

Human teeth scored his skin, pushing Rex over the edge as his mate's seed filled him.

Aaron's softening dick slipped out, and Rex rolled to face him. Long fingers caressed the side of his face. His mate's hazel eyes were huge.

"I thought I was happy. I had my music and believed it was all I needed. But there was a hole, here." He touched his chest. "Now, you're there."

"Oh, babe." A part of Rex wondered how in the hell he'd been worthy enough to warrant such a mate. He drew Aaron close and held him tight. "*Mi corazón.*" For his mate was his heart.

Aaron snuggled against him and mirrored his response in Italian. "*Il mio cuore.*"

About the Author

V.S. Morgan has lived all over the US but calls Minnesota her home now. She's been writing stories since she could hold a pencil and dreams of happily ever afters - even for two hot men - because love knows no boundaries. V.S. writes IRMC contemporary, paranormal, and suspense m/m and m/f with heart.

Also by V.S. Morgan

Hunter's Mark
Sam's Temptation
The Gift